# JACK AN OX

TAP! TAP!

### A TOON BOOK BY
### art spiegelman

# WINNER OF THE WHITE RAVEN AWARD
# BANK STREET COLLEGE'S BEST CHILDREN'S BOOK OF THE YEAR
# PW'S BEST CHILDREN'S PICTURE BOOKS
# GRAPHIC NOVEL REPORTER'S CORE LIST OF GRAPHIC NOVELS FOR KIDS

Editorial Director: FRANÇOISE MOULY
Advisor: ART SPIEGELMAN

Book Design: FRANÇOISE MOULY, JONATHAN BENNETT & ART SPIEGELMAN
ART SPIEGELMAN'S artwork was done in India ink and colored digitally.

A TOON Book™ © 2008 RAW Junior, LLC, 27 Greene Street, New York, NY 10013. No part of this book may be used or reproduced in any manner whatsoever without written permission except in the case of brief quotations embodied in critical articles and reviews. TOON Graphics™, TOON Books®, LITTLE LIT® and TOON Into Reading!™ are trademarks of RAW Junior, LLC. All our books are Smyth Sewn (the highest library-quality binding available) and printed with soy-based inks on acid-free, woodfree paper harvested from responsible sources. Printed in China by C&C Offset Printing Co., Ltd. Distributed to the trade by Consortium Book Sales & Distribution, a division of Ingram Content Group; orders (866) 400-5351; ips@ingramcontent.com; www.cbsd.com. Library of Congress Control Number: 200791034

ISBN 978-0-9799238-3-8 (hardcover)    ISBN 978-1-935179-30-6 (paperback)

19 20 21 22 23 24 C&C 10 9 8 7 6 5 4 3

www.TOON-BOOKS.com

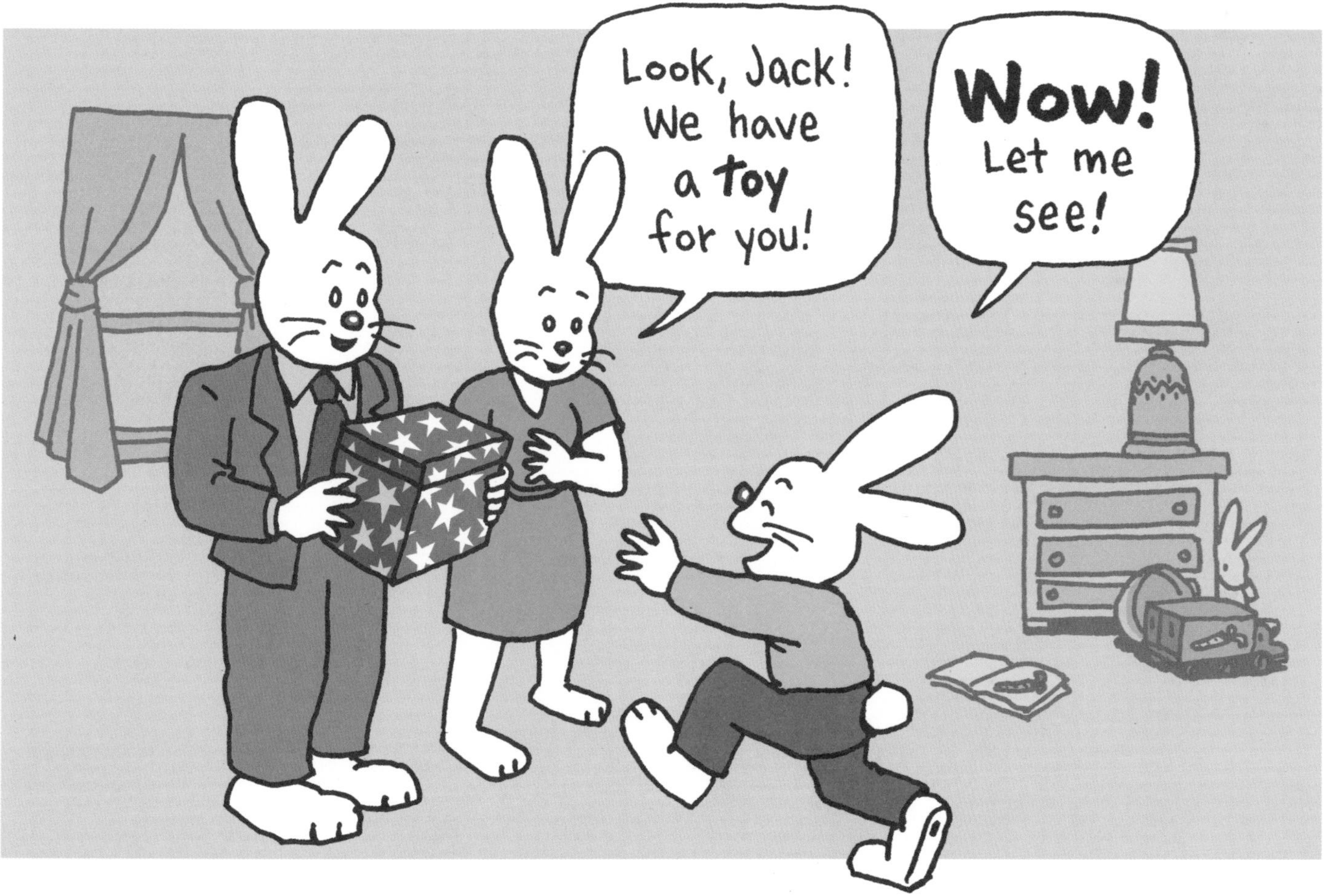
Look, Jack! We have a **toy** for you!
**Wow!** Let me see!

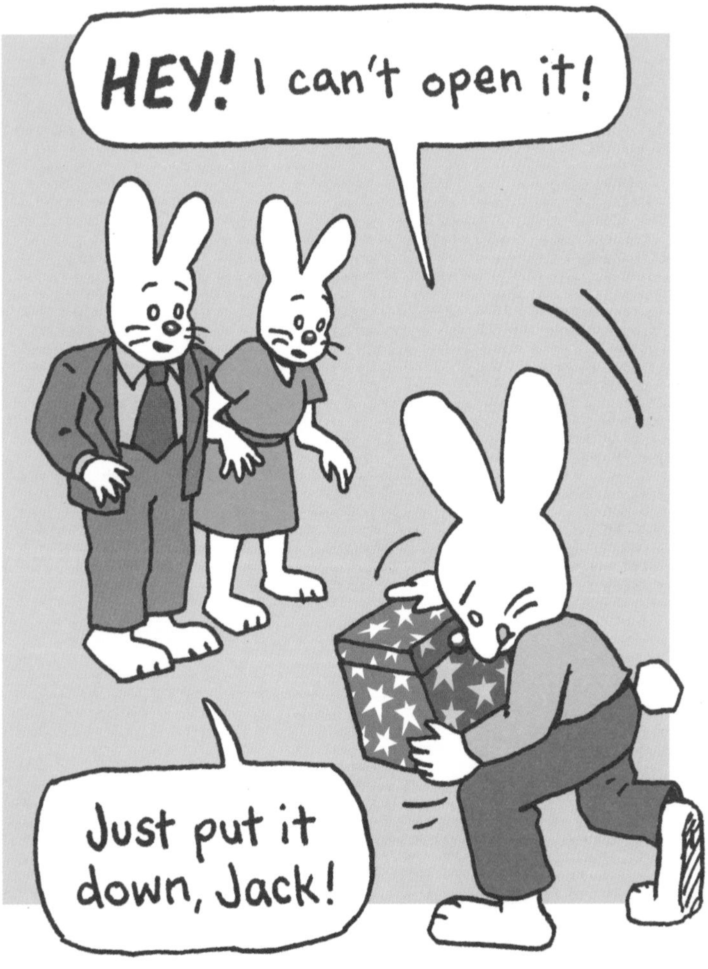
HEY! I can't open it!
Just put it down, Jack!

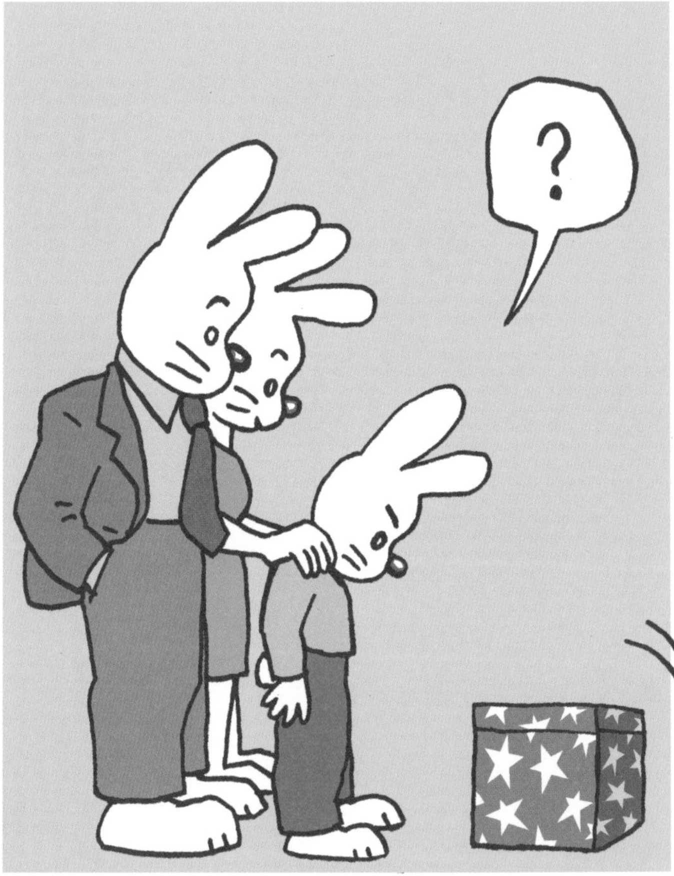
?

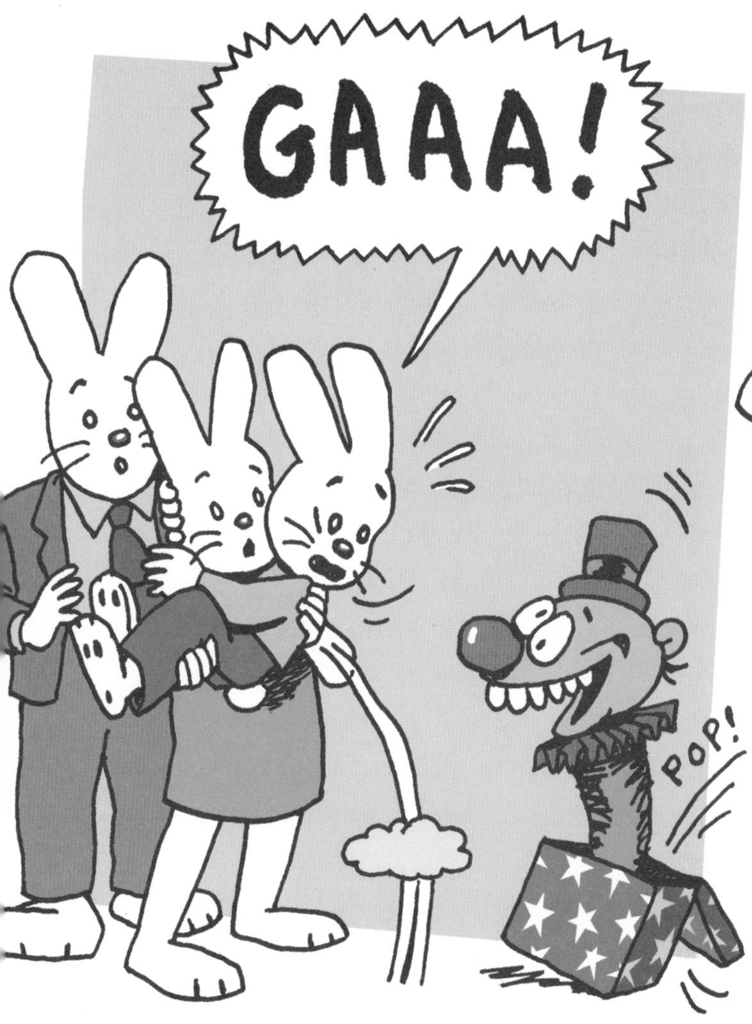
GAAA!
POP!

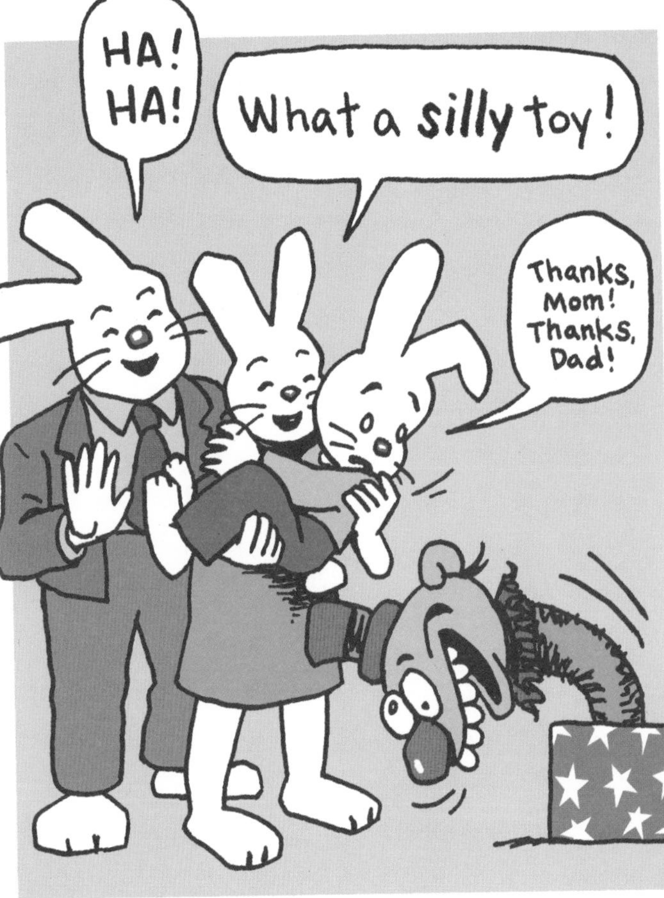
HA! HA!
What a silly toy!
Thanks, Mom! Thanks, Dad!

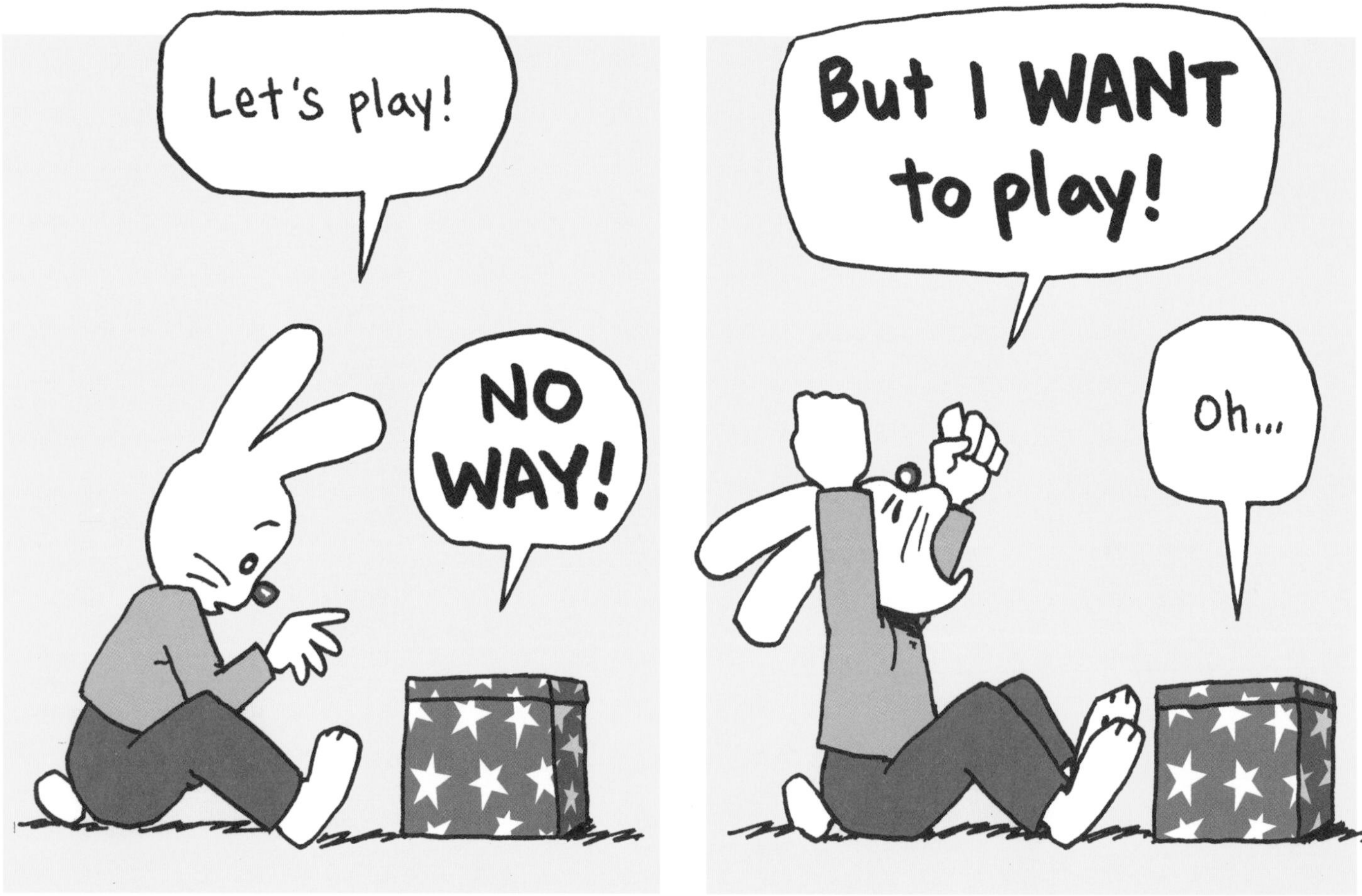
Let's play!
NO WAY!
But I WANT to play!
Oh...

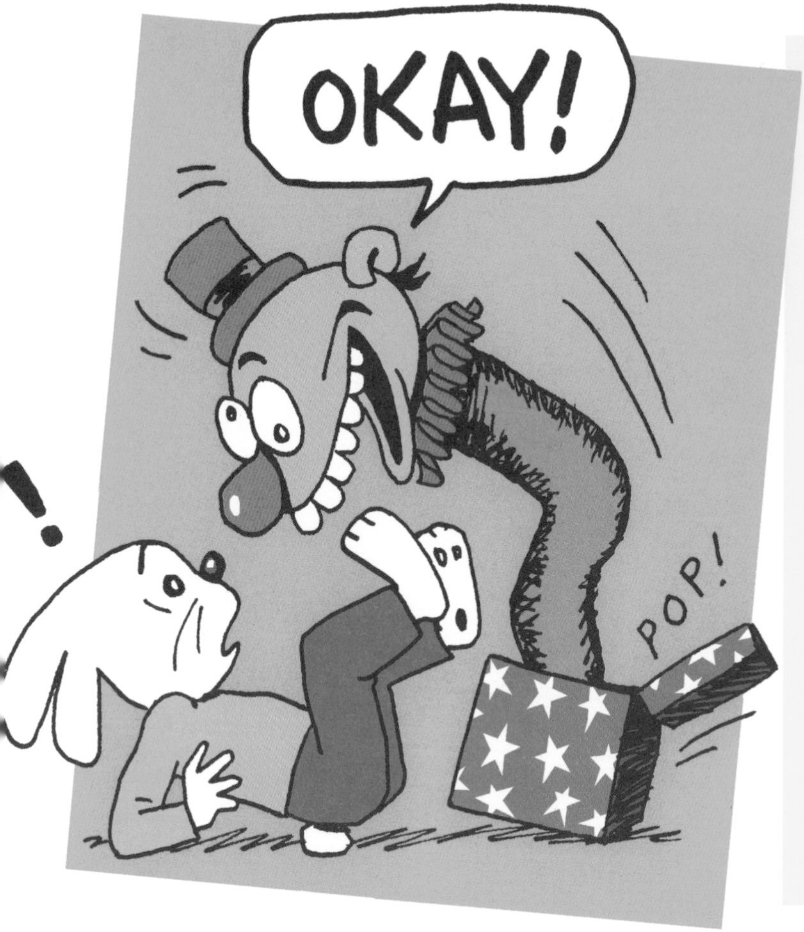
!
OKAY!
POP!

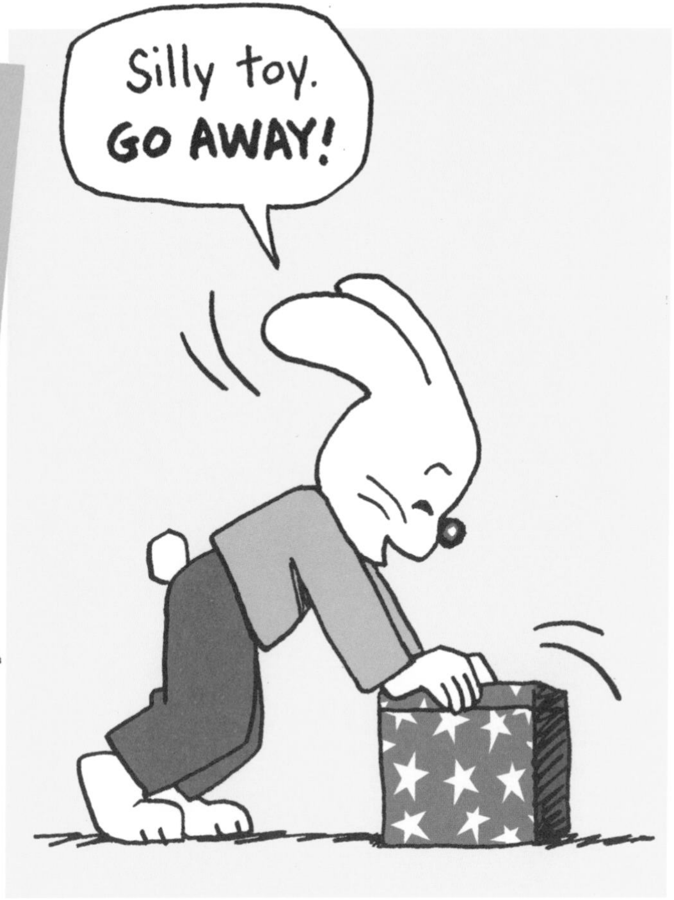
Silly toy.
GO AWAY!

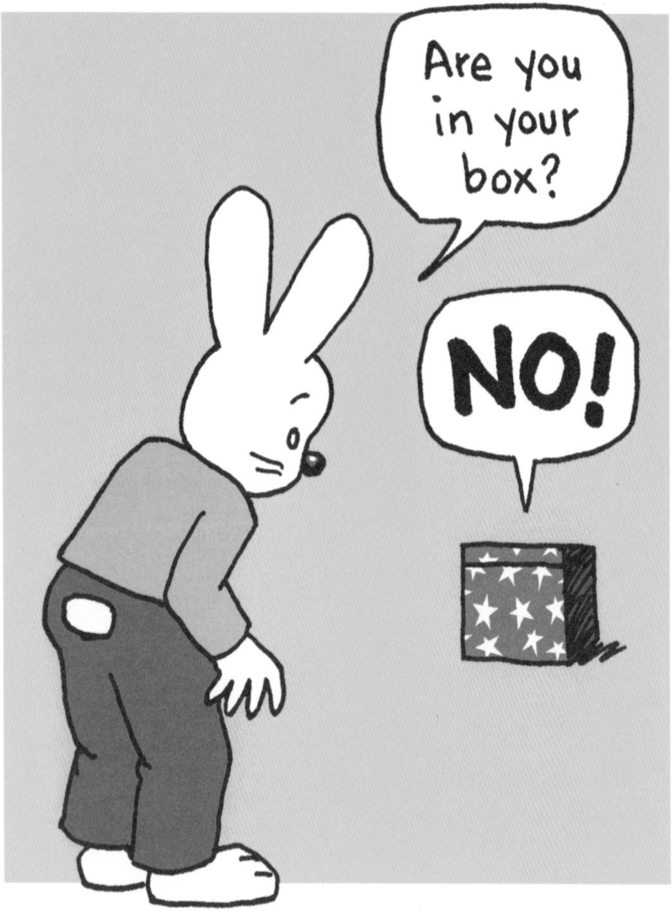

Are you in your box?
NO!

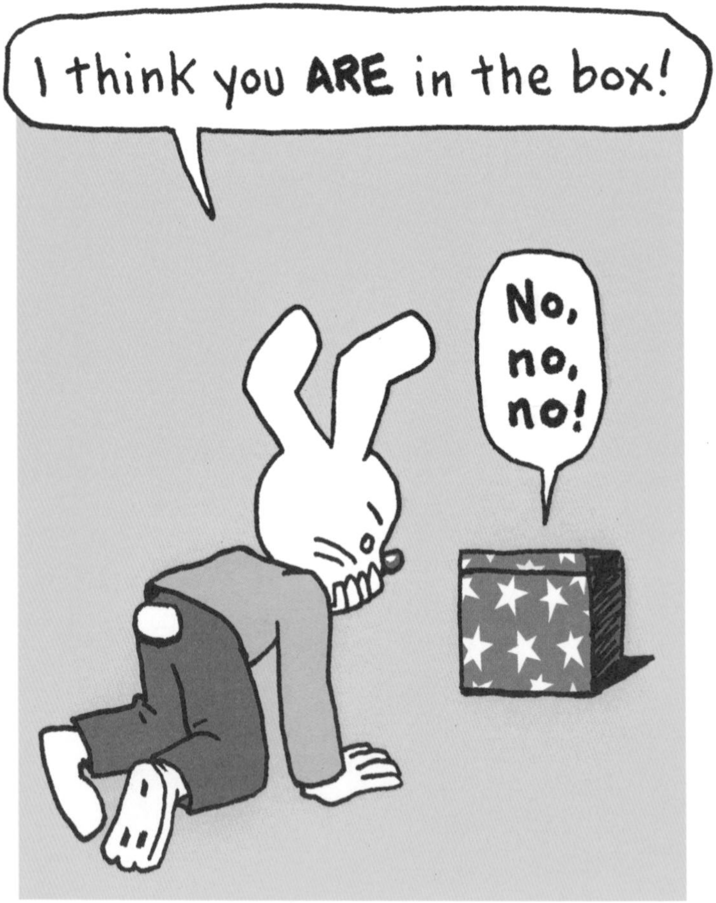

I think you **ARE** in the box!
No, no, no!

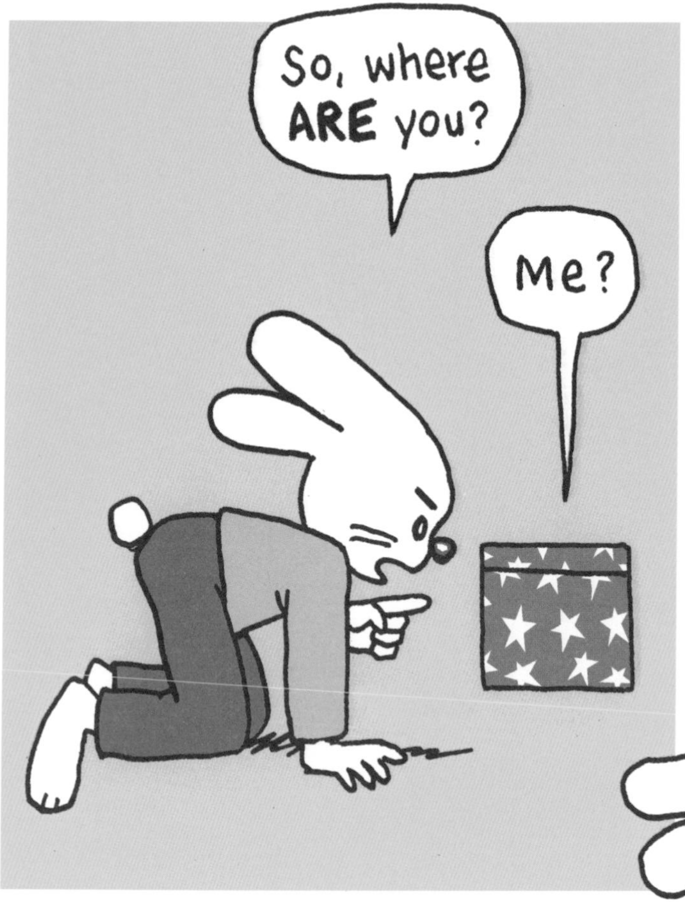
So, where ARE you?
Me?

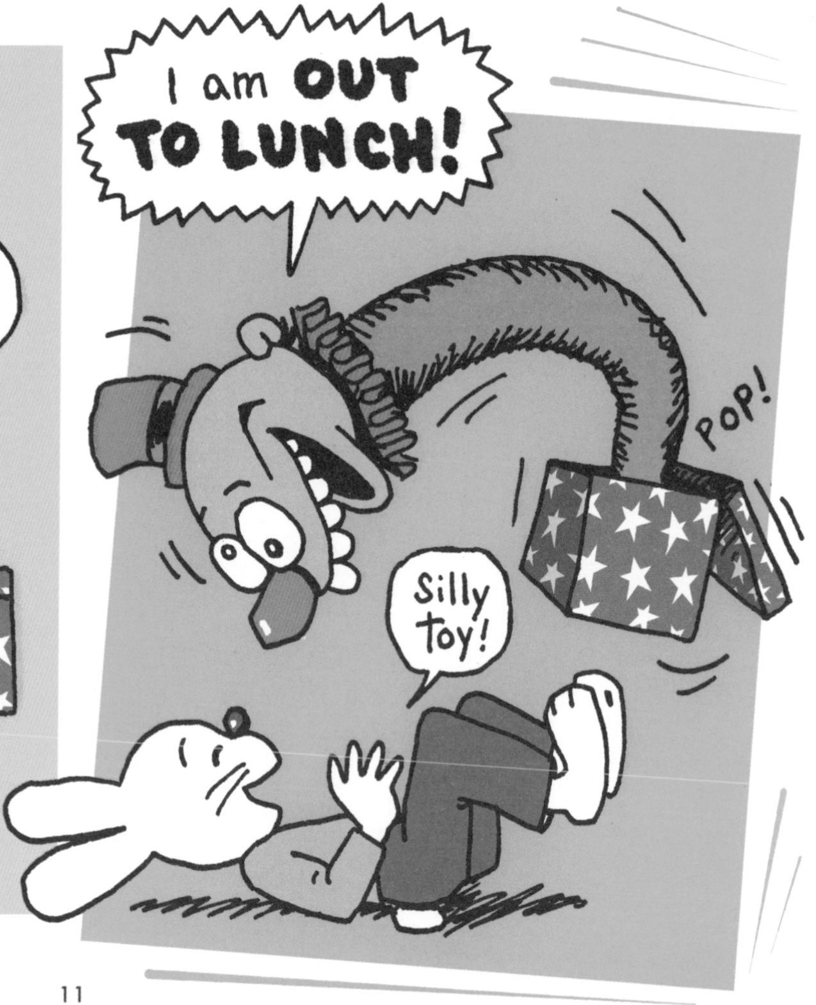
I am OUT TO LUNCH!
POP!
Silly Toy!

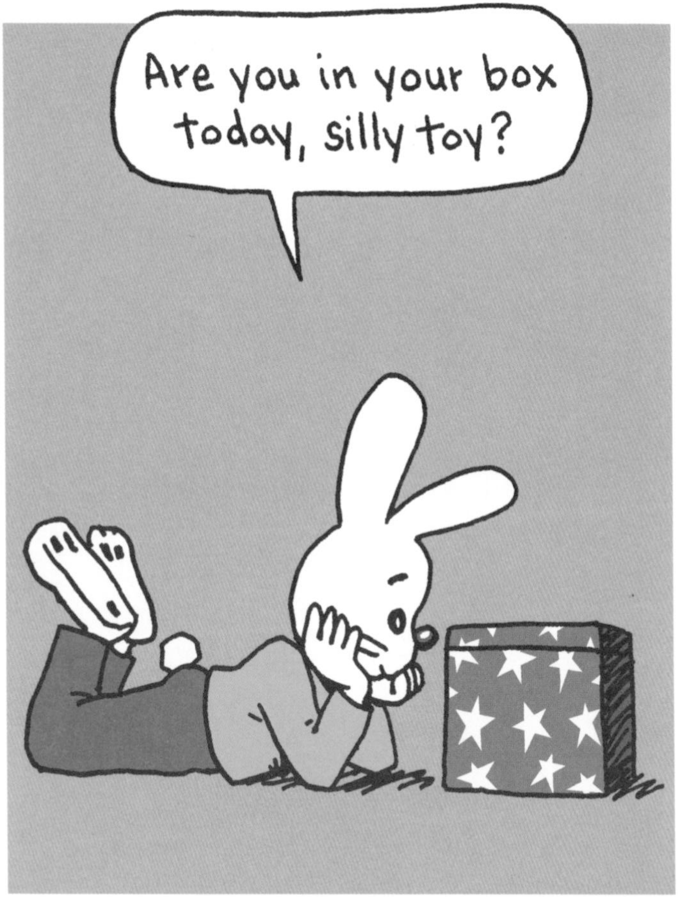
Are you in your box today, silly toy?

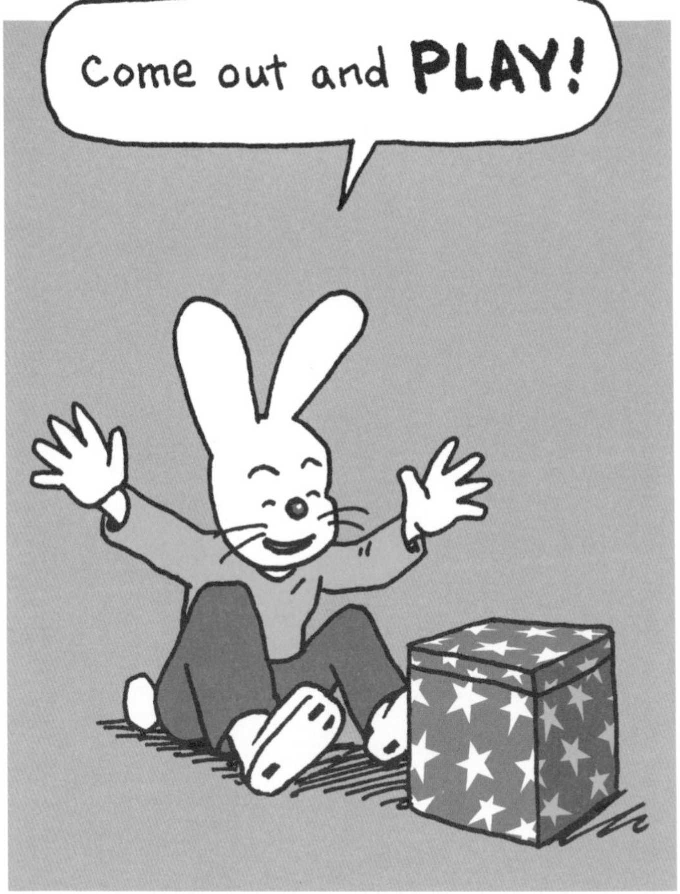
Come out and PLAY!

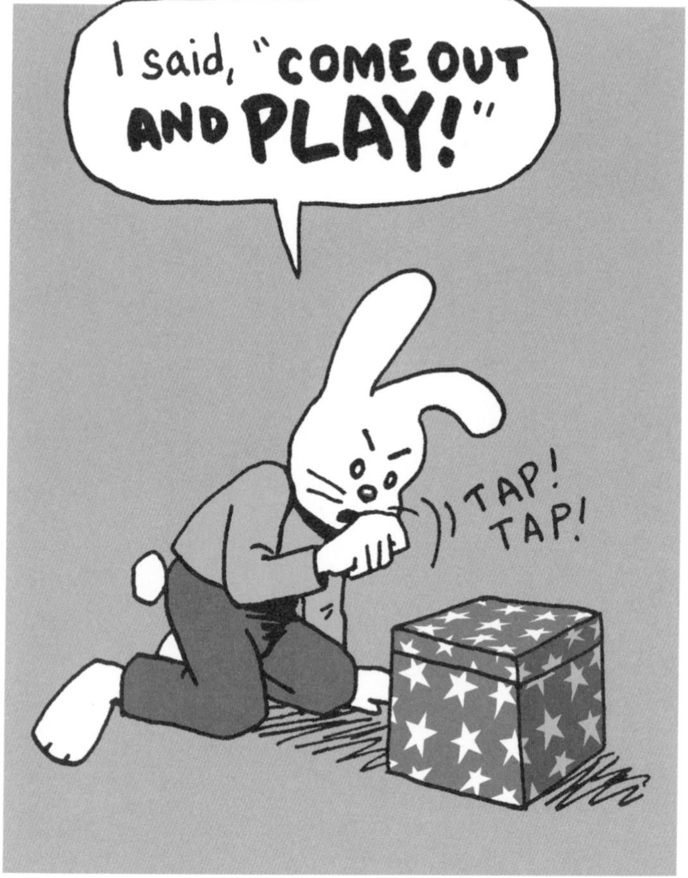
I said, "COME OUT AND PLAY!"
TAP! TAP!

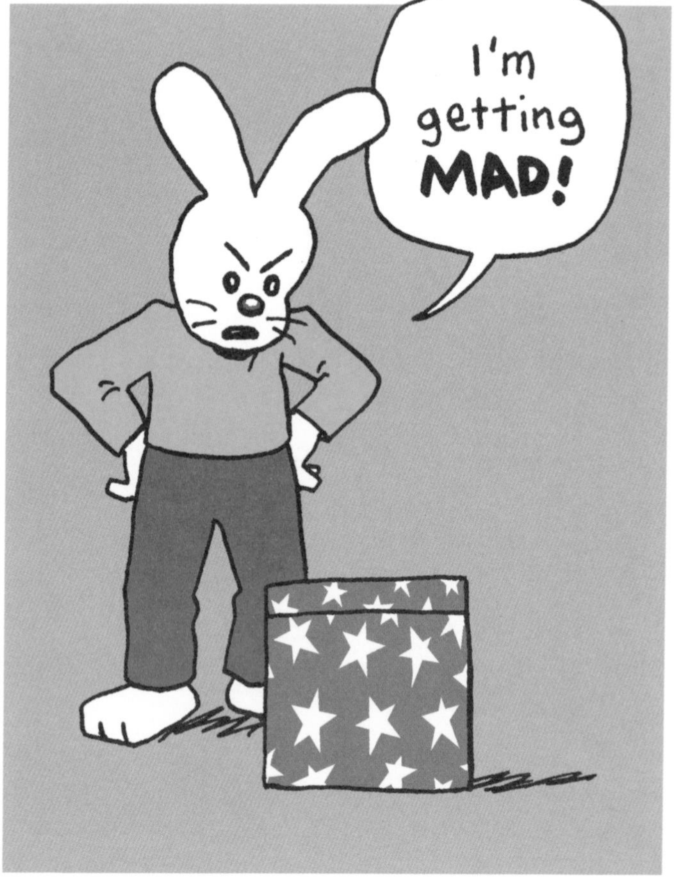
I'm getting MAD!

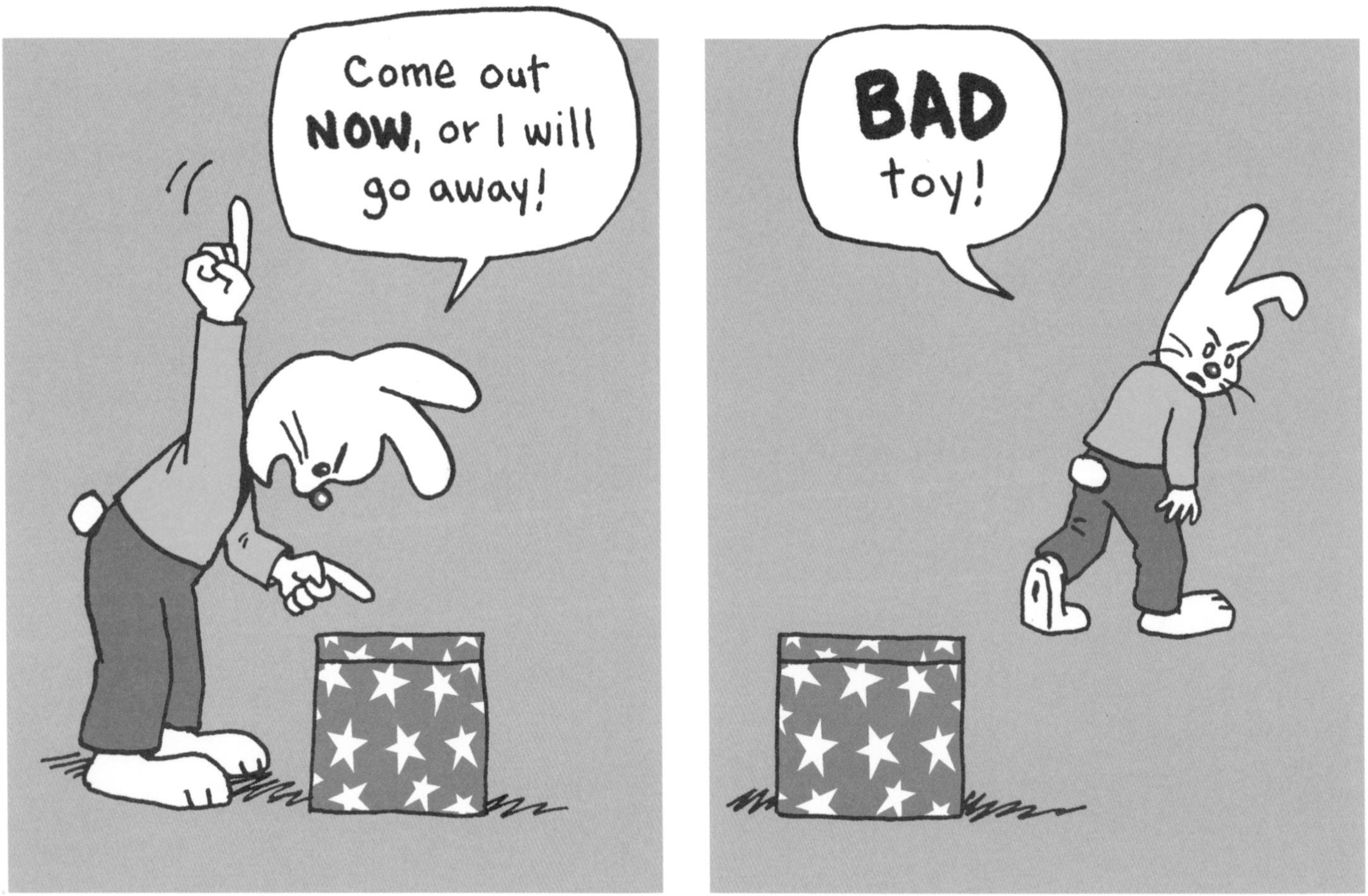
Come out **NOW**, or I will go away!
**BAD** toy!

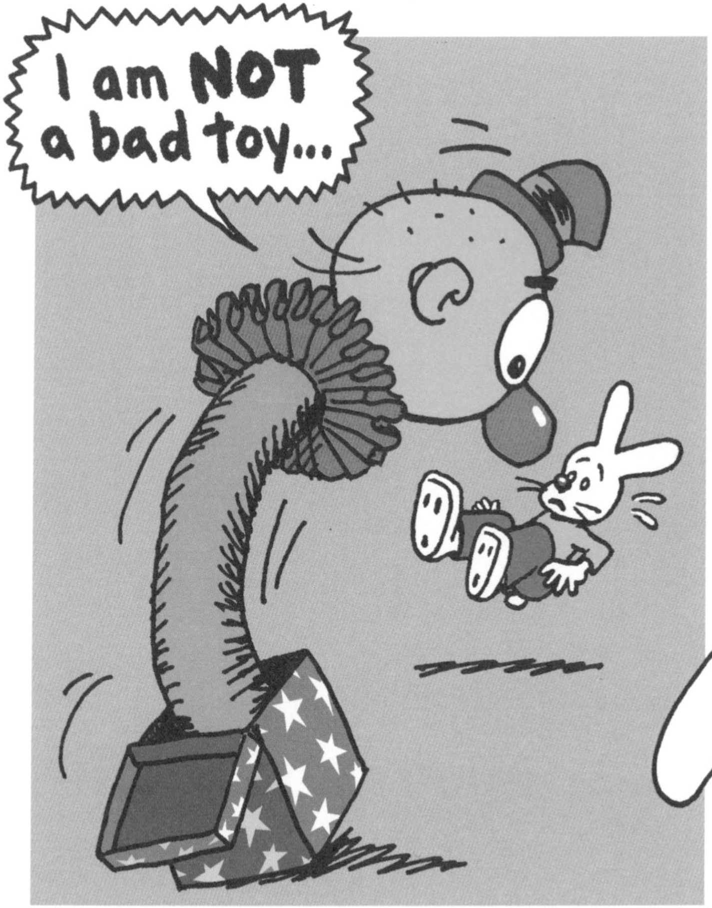
I am NOT a bad toy...

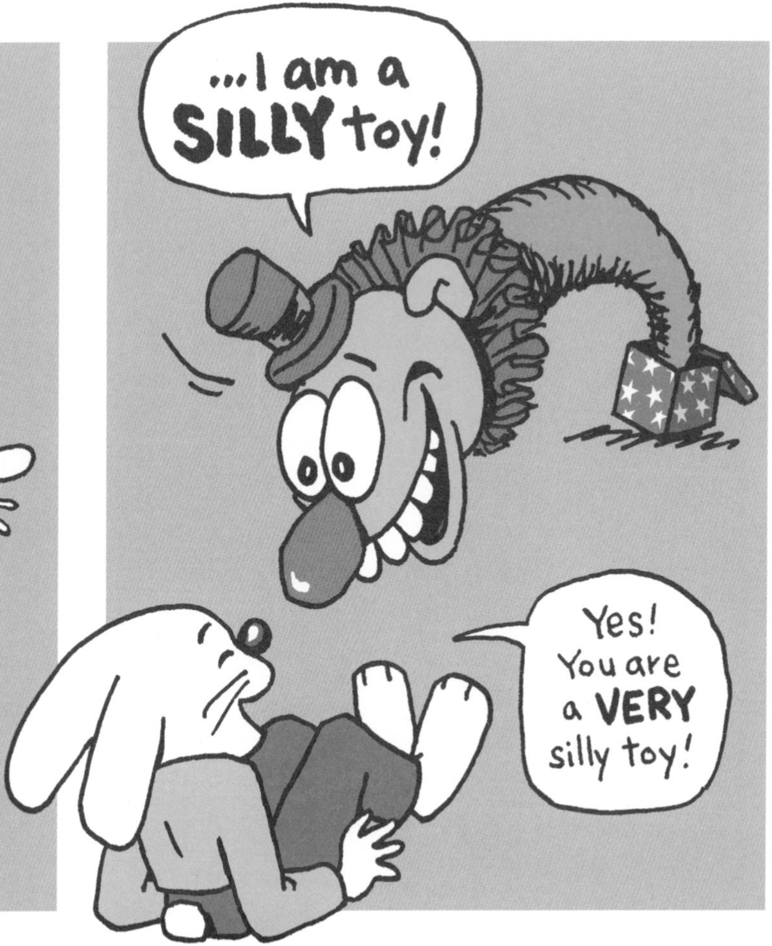
...I am a SILLY toy!
Yes! You are a VERY silly toy!

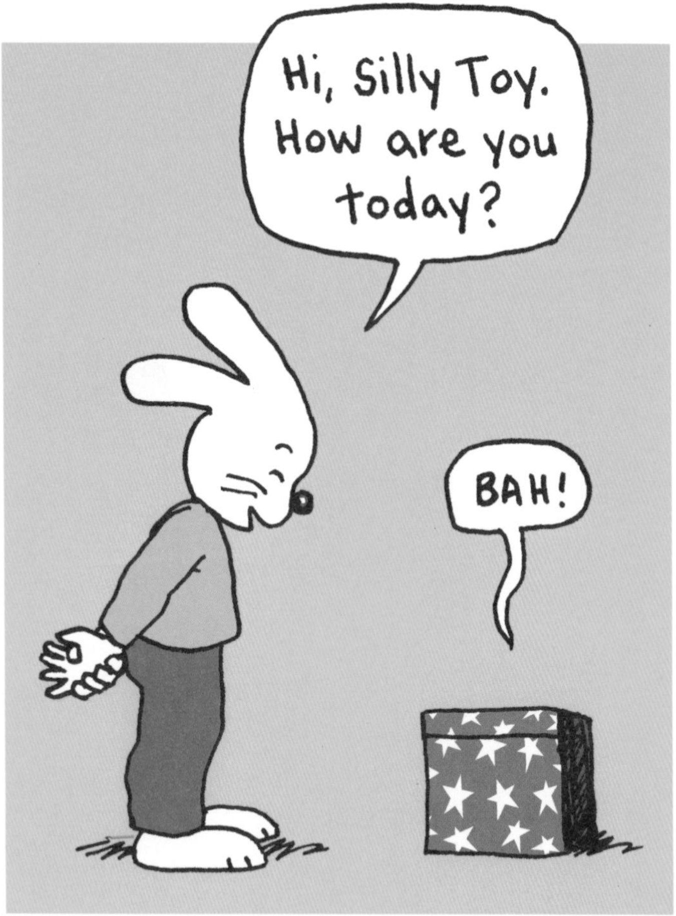
Hi, Silly Toy. How are you today?
BAH!

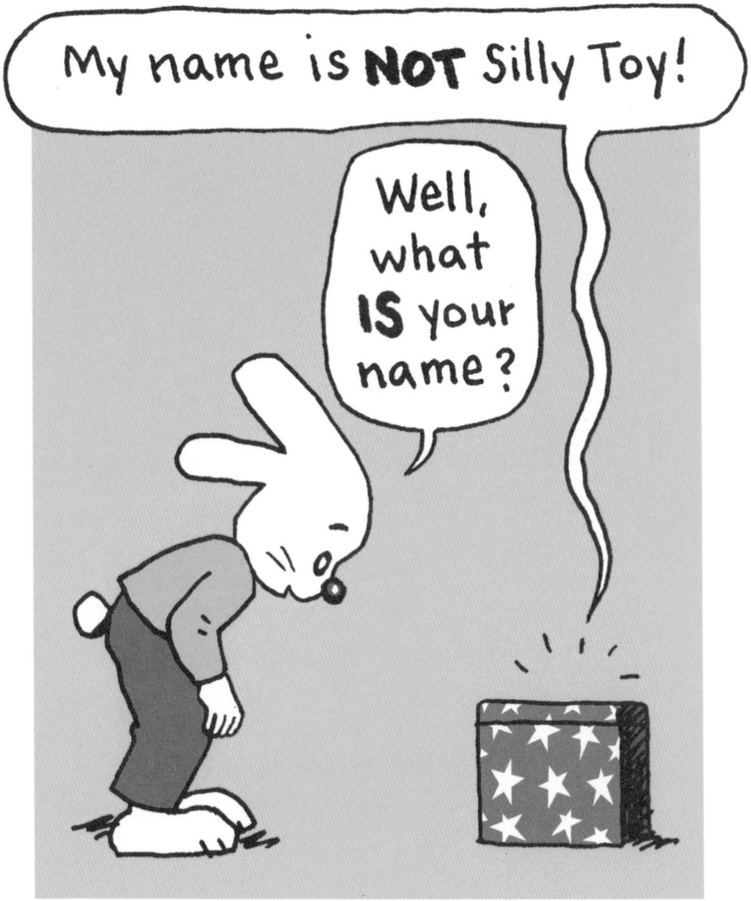
My name is **NOT** Silly Toy!
Well, what **IS** your name?

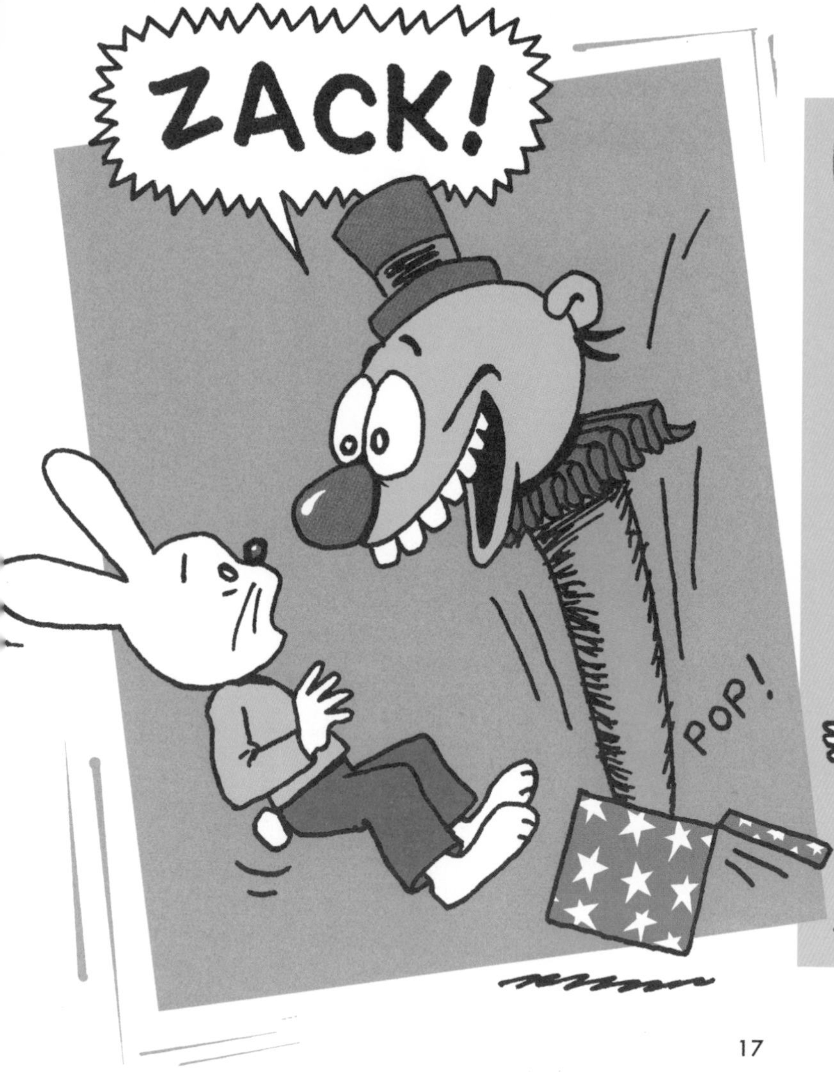
ZACK!
POP!

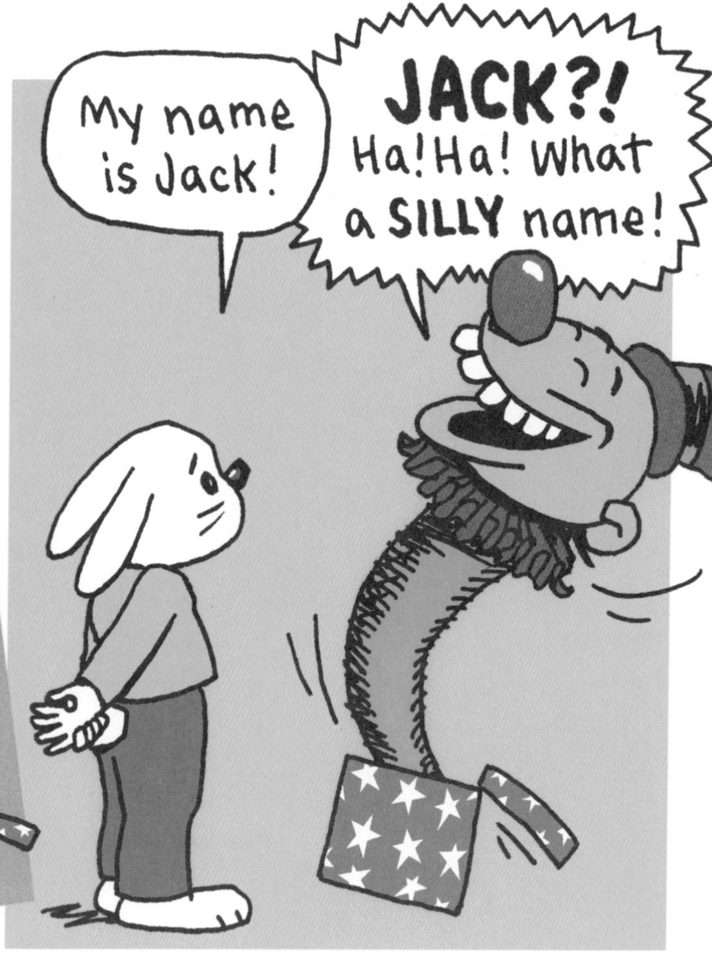
My name is Jack!
JACK?! Ha! Ha! What a SILLY name!

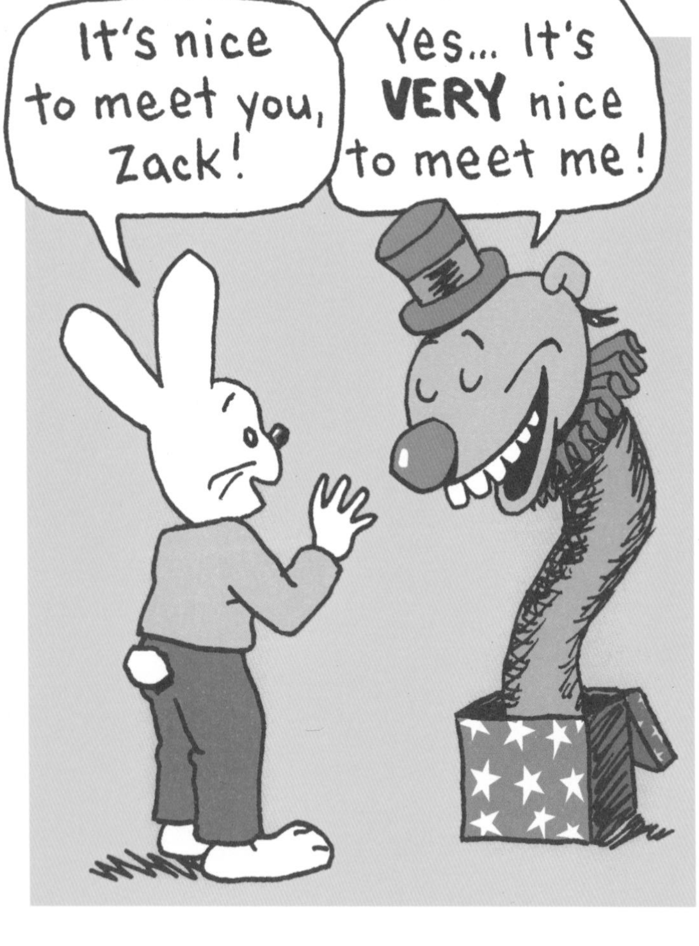
It's nice to meet you, Zack!
Yes... It's VERY nice to meet me!

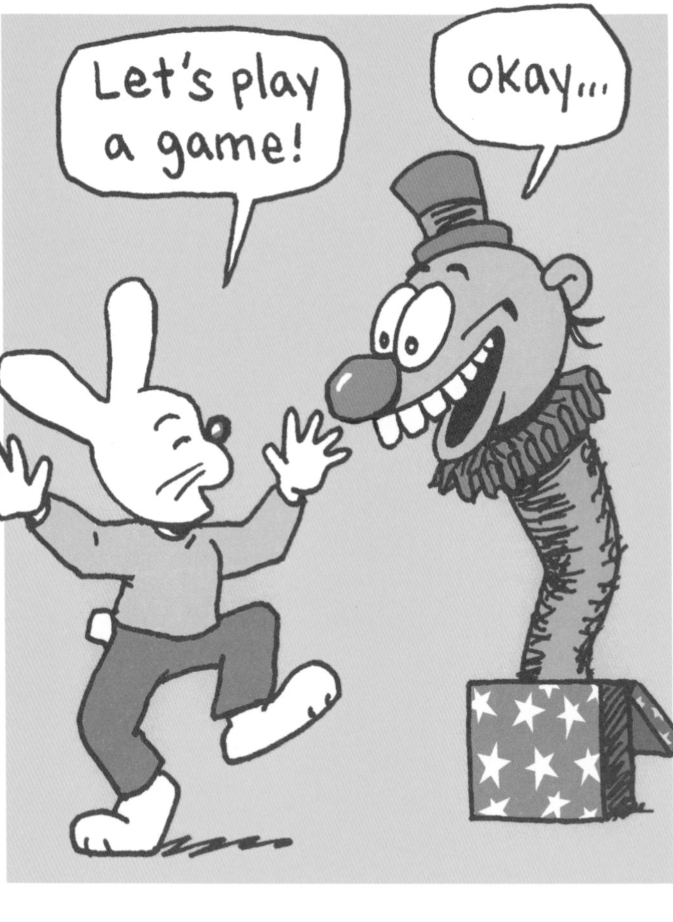
Let's play a game!
okay...

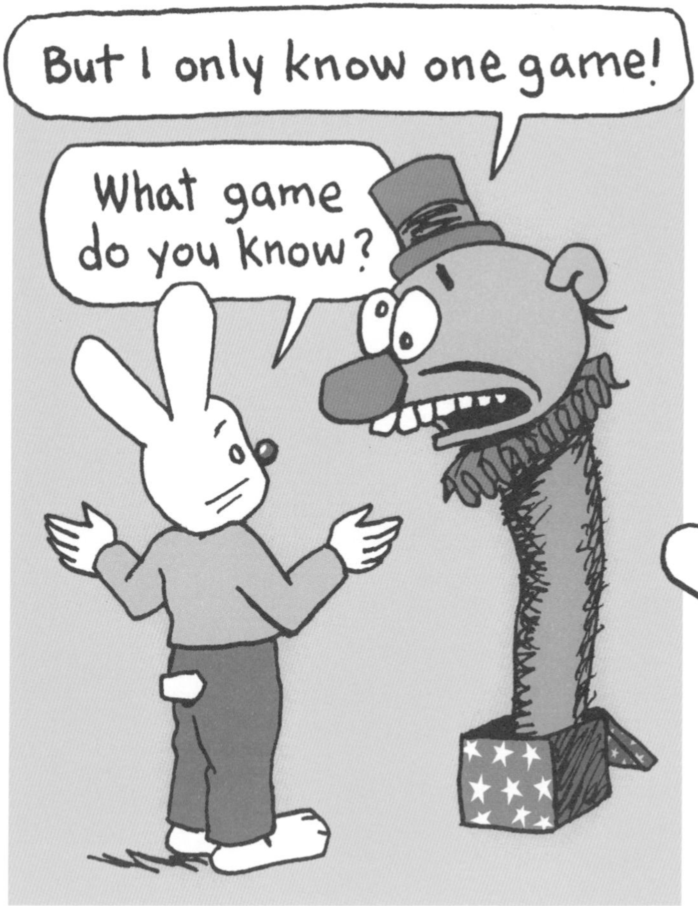
What game do you know?
But I only know one game!

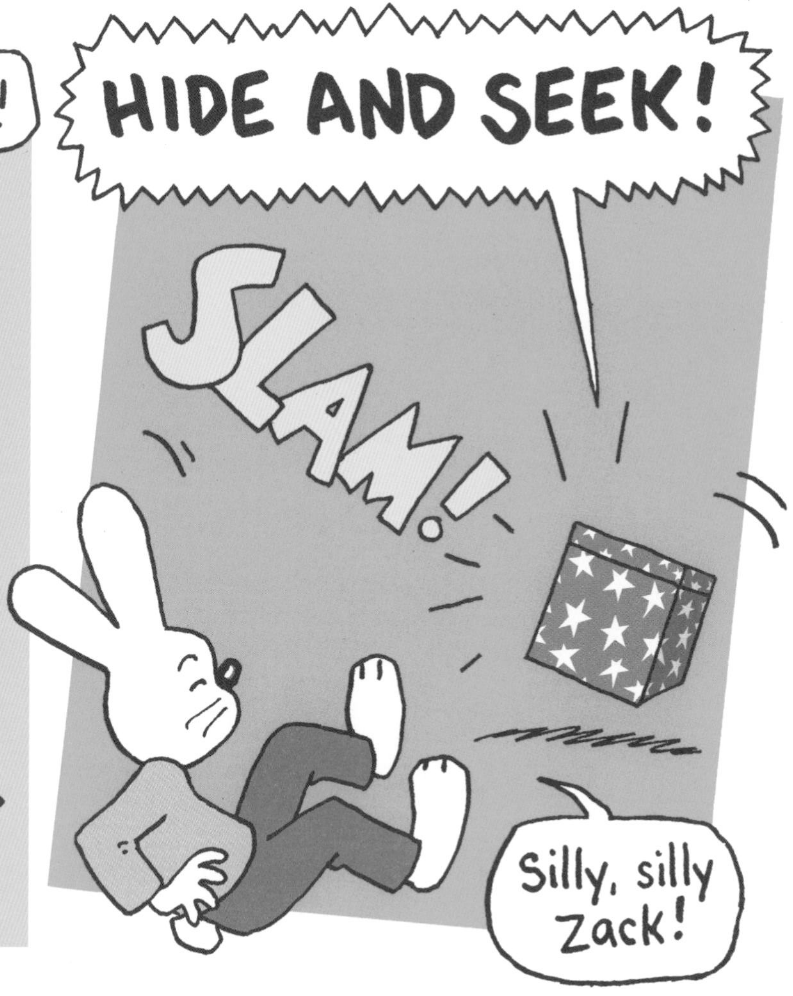
HIDE AND SEEK!
SLAM!
Silly, silly Zack!

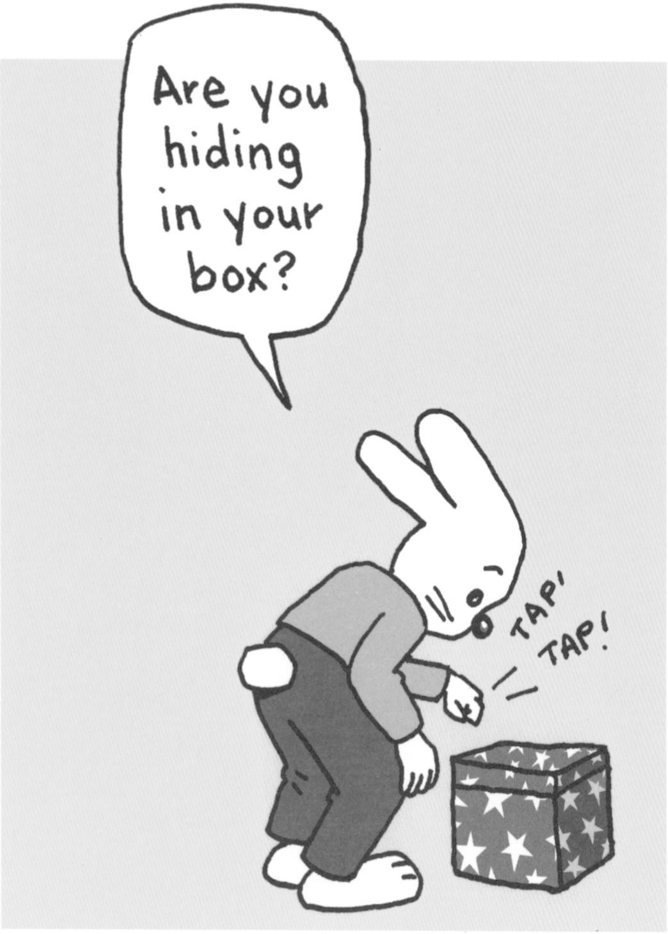
Are you hiding in your box?
TAP! TAP!

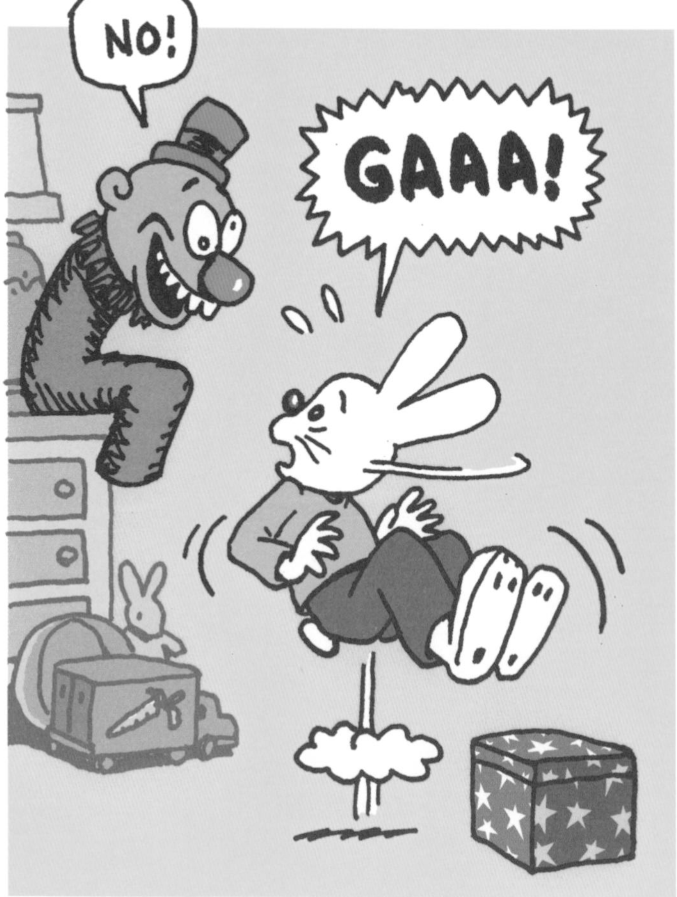
NO!
GAAA!

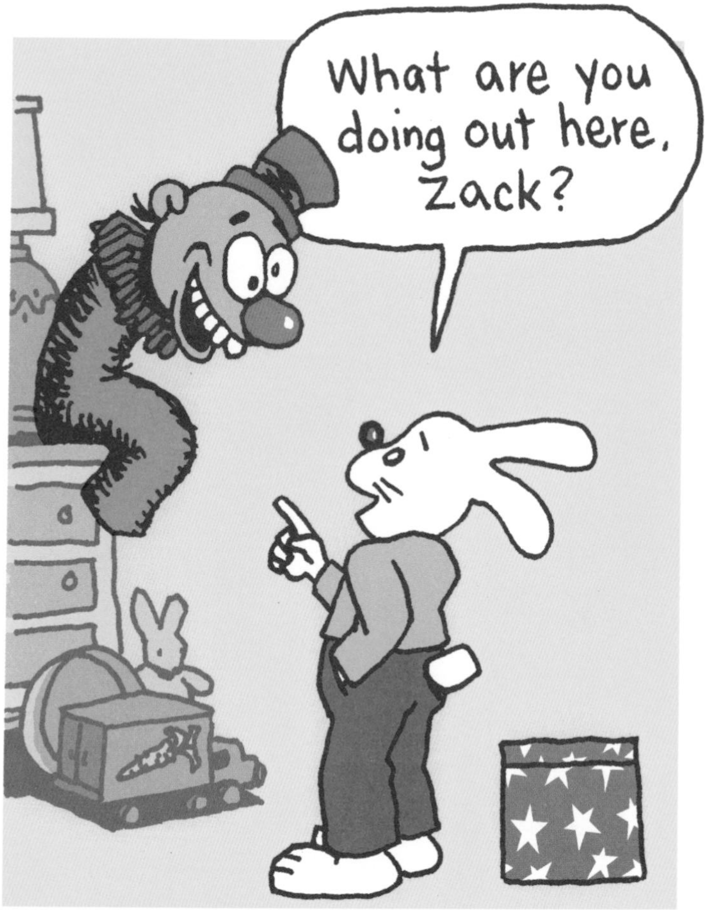
What are you doing out here, Zack?

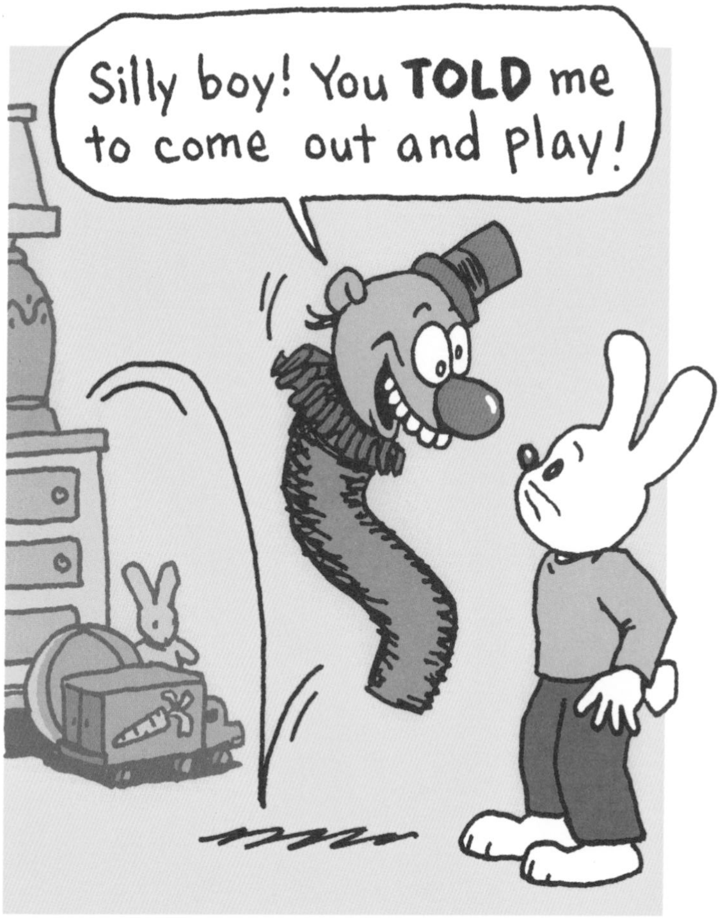
Silly boy! You TOLD me to come out and play!

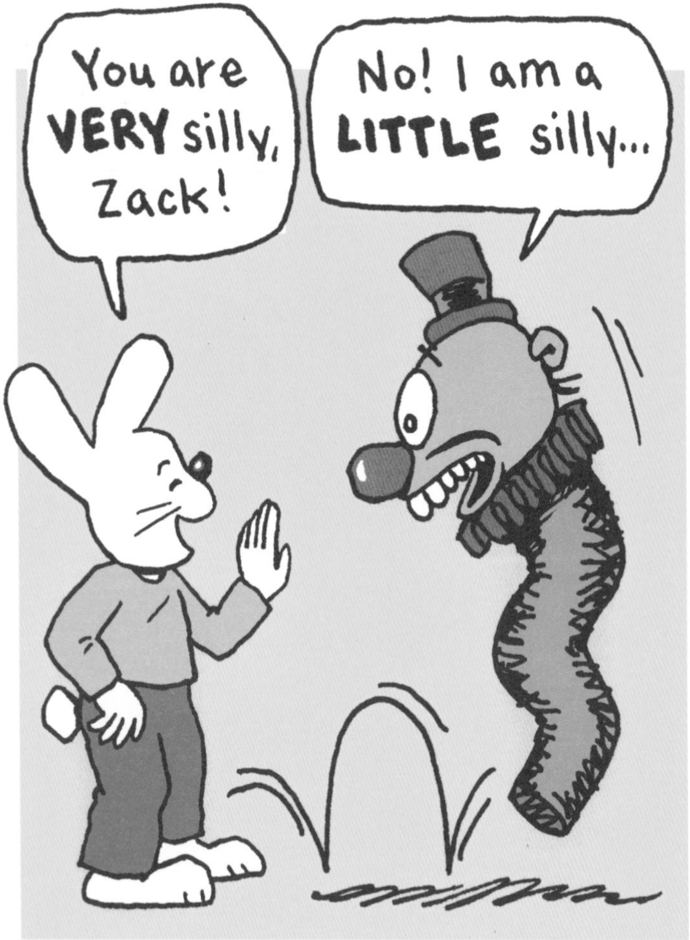
You are **VERY** silly, Zack!
No! I am a **LITTLE** silly...

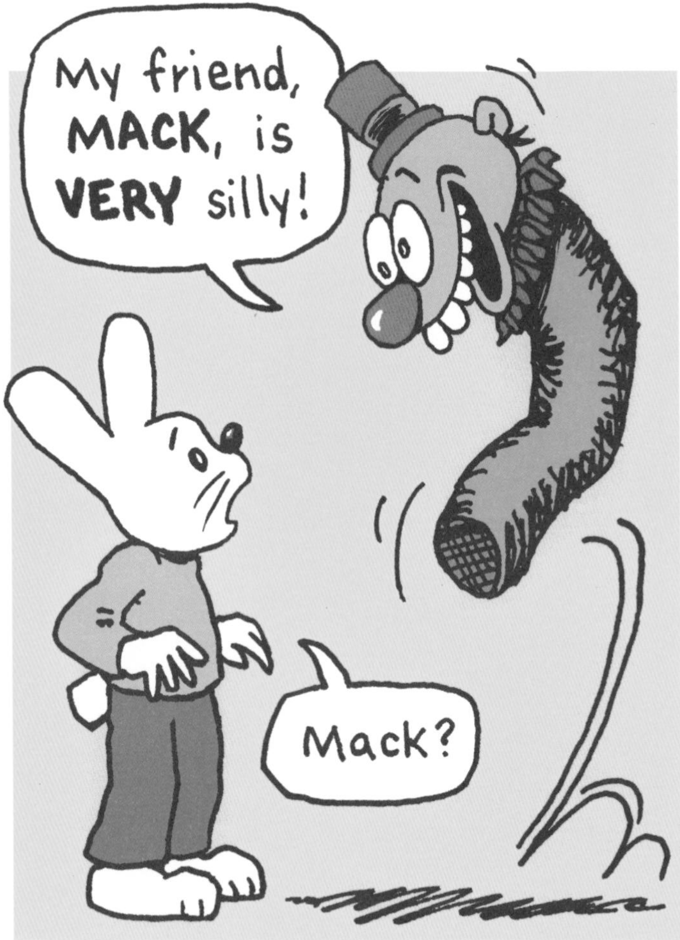
My friend, **MACK**, is **VERY** silly!
Mack?

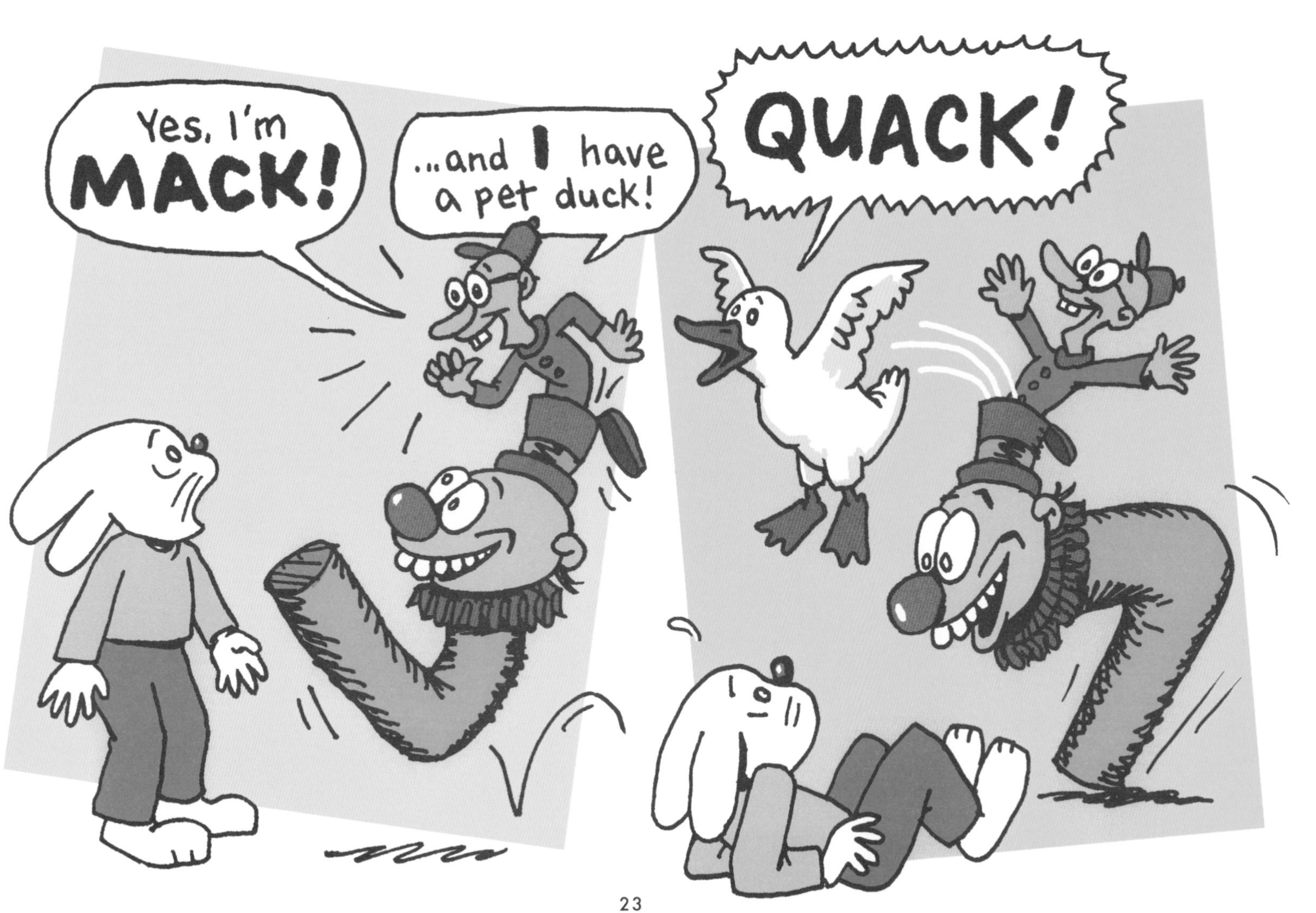
Yes, I'm MACK!
...and I have a pet duck!
QUACK!

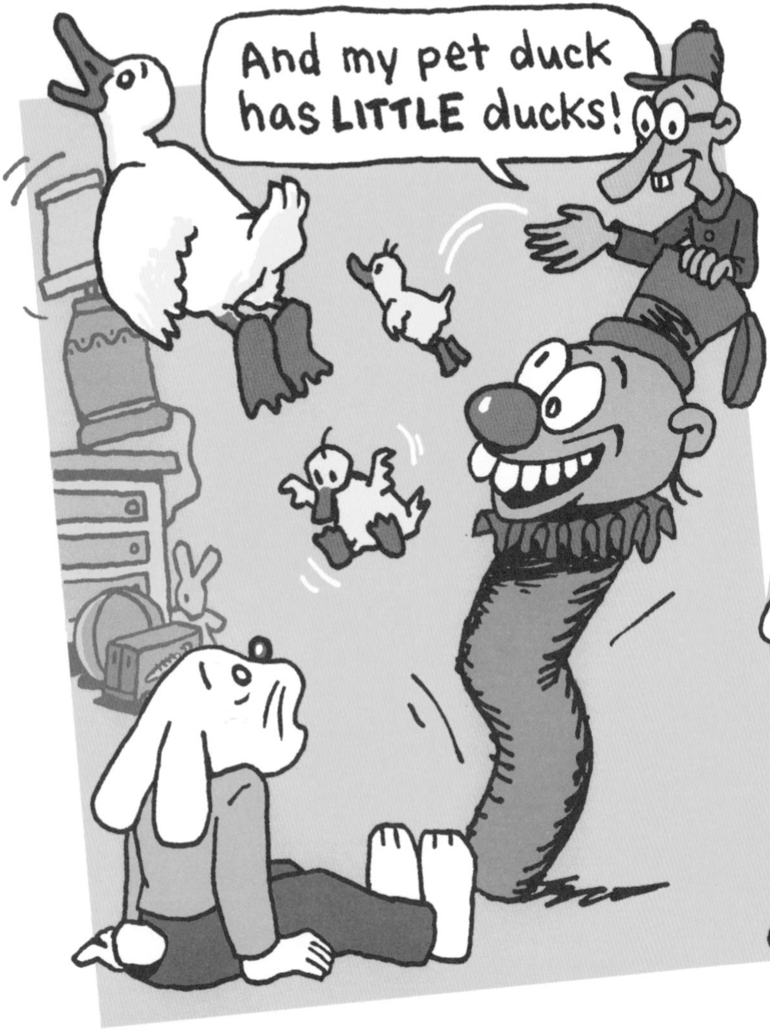
And my pet duck has LITTLE ducks!

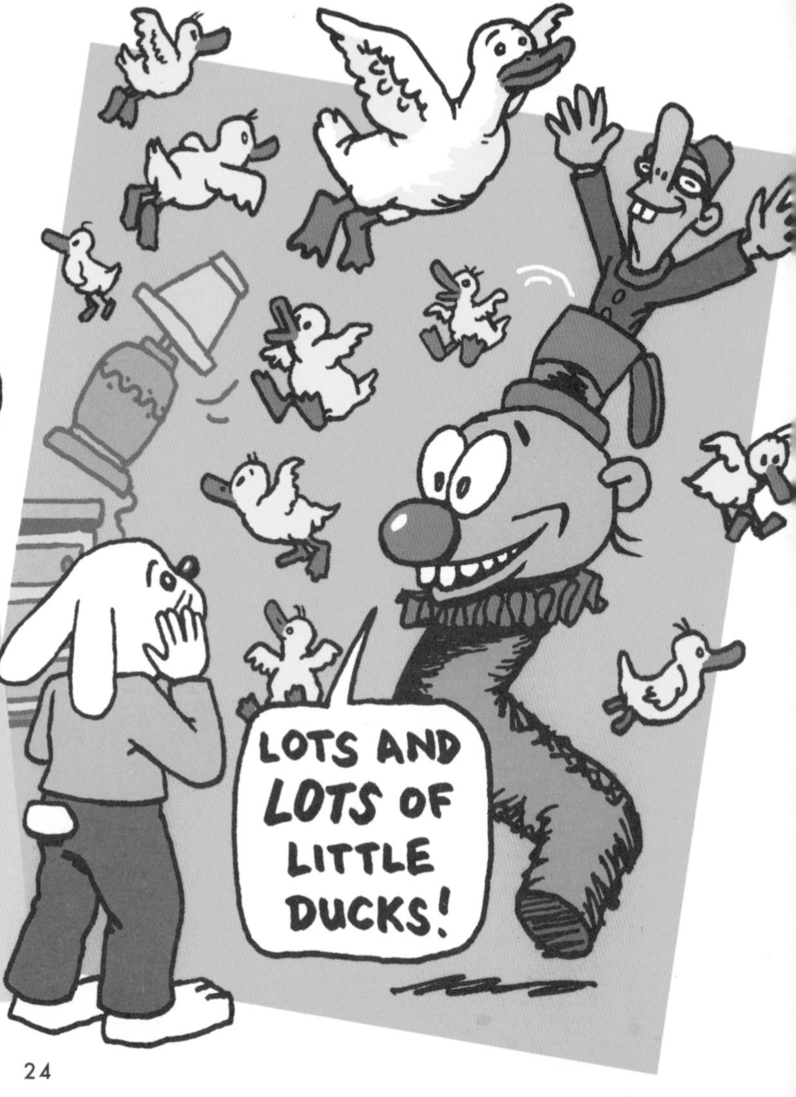
LOTS AND LOTS OF LITTLE DUCKS!

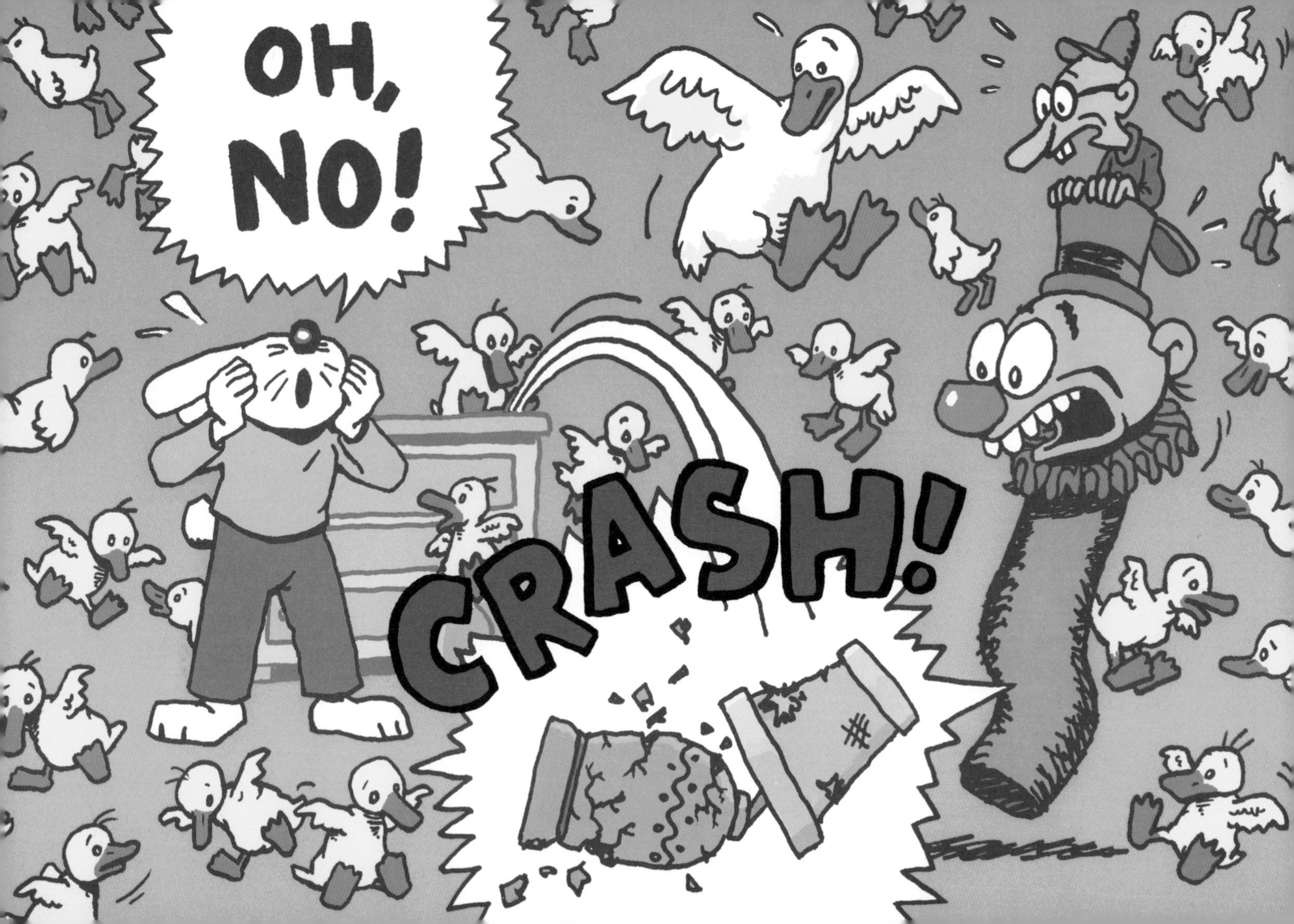
OH, NO!
CRASH!

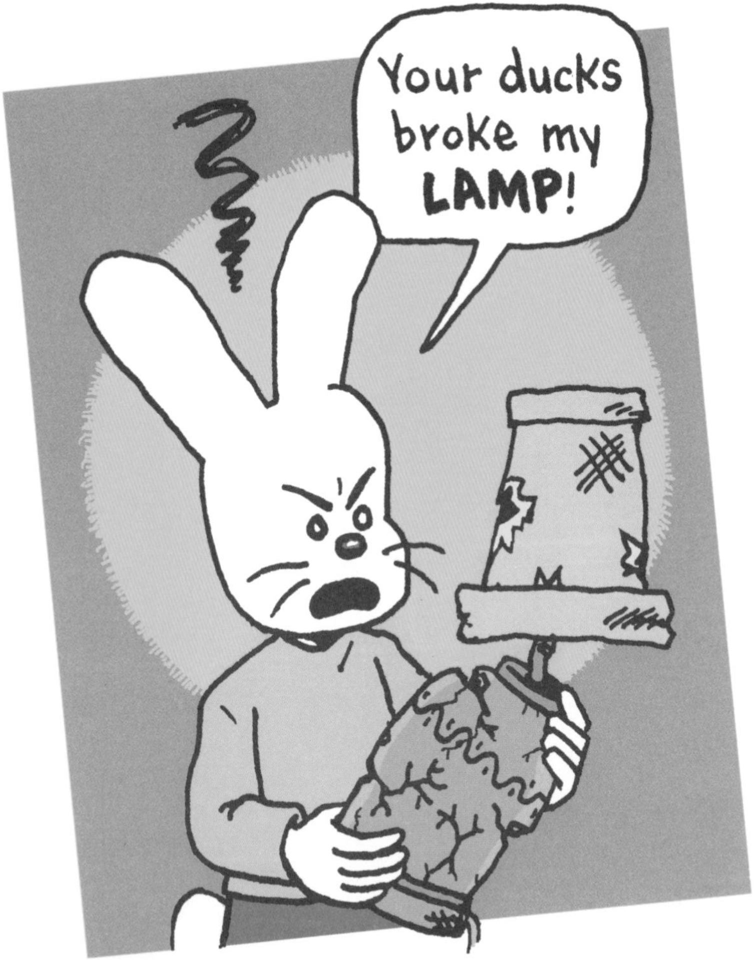
Your ducks broke my LAMP!

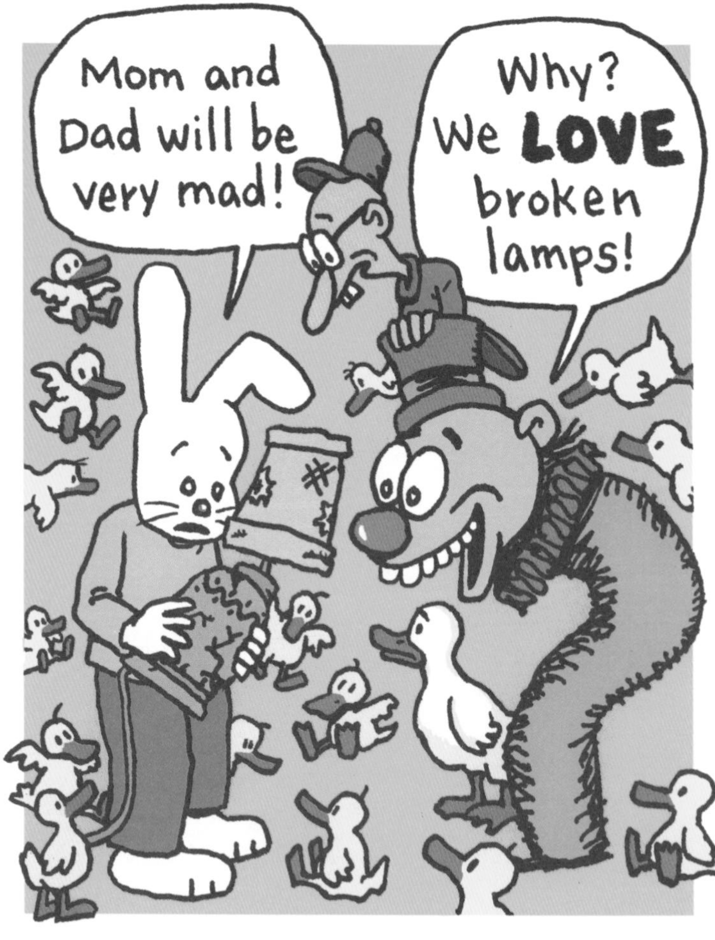
Mom and Dad will be very mad!
Why? We LOVE broken lamps!

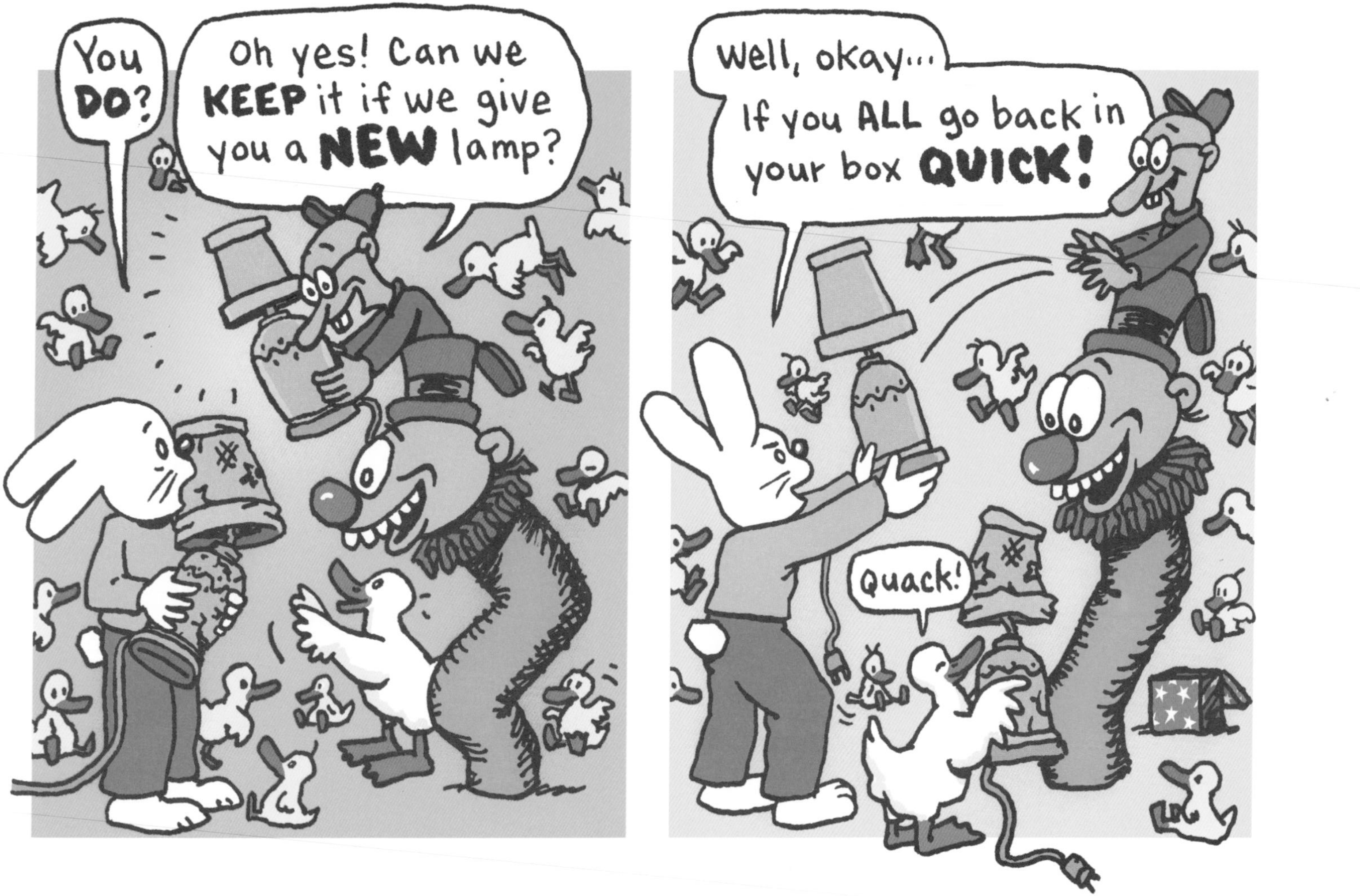
You **DO**?
Oh yes! Can we **KEEP** it if we give you a **NEW** lamp?
Well, okay...
If you **ALL** go back in your box **QUICK!**
Quack!

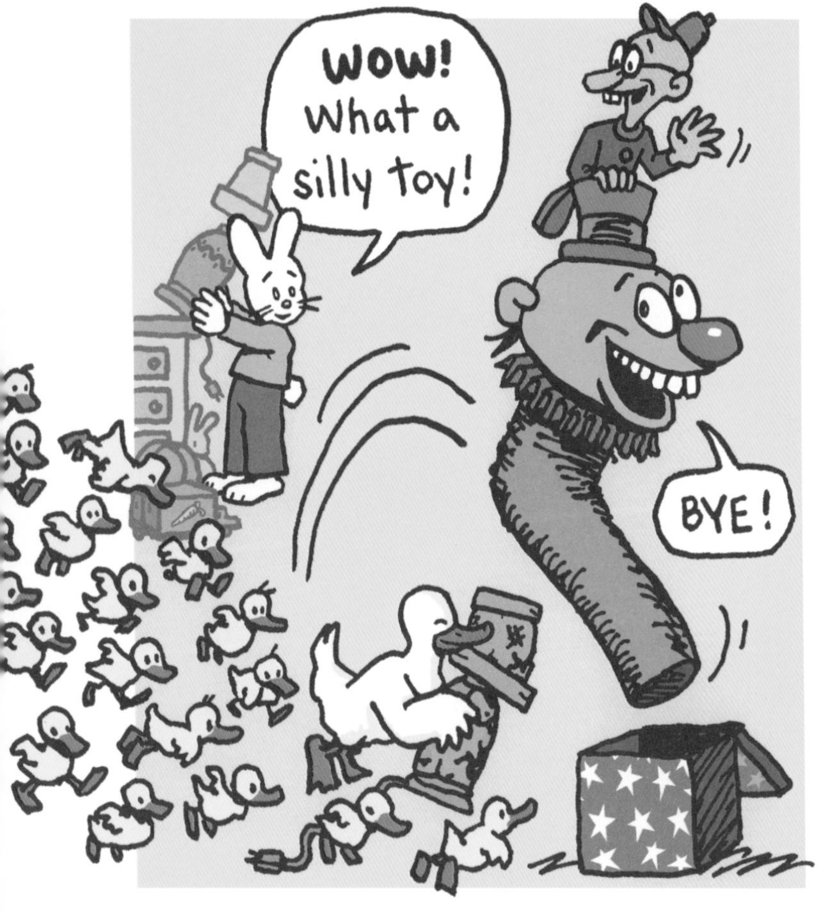
WOW! What a silly toy!
BYE!

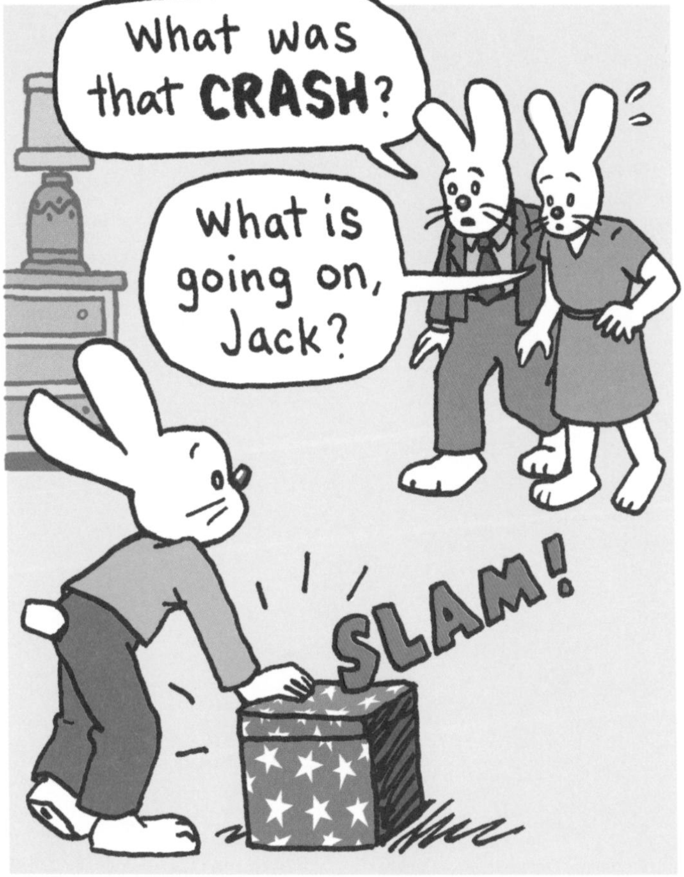
What was that CRASH?
What is going on, Jack?
SLAM!

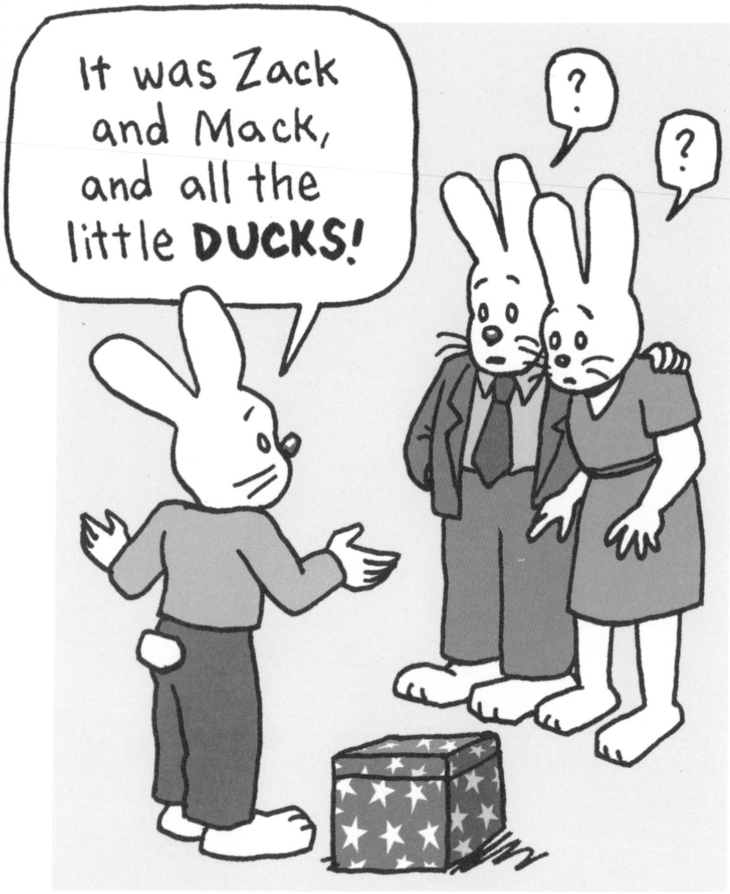
It was Zack and Mack, and all the little **DUCKS!**
?
?

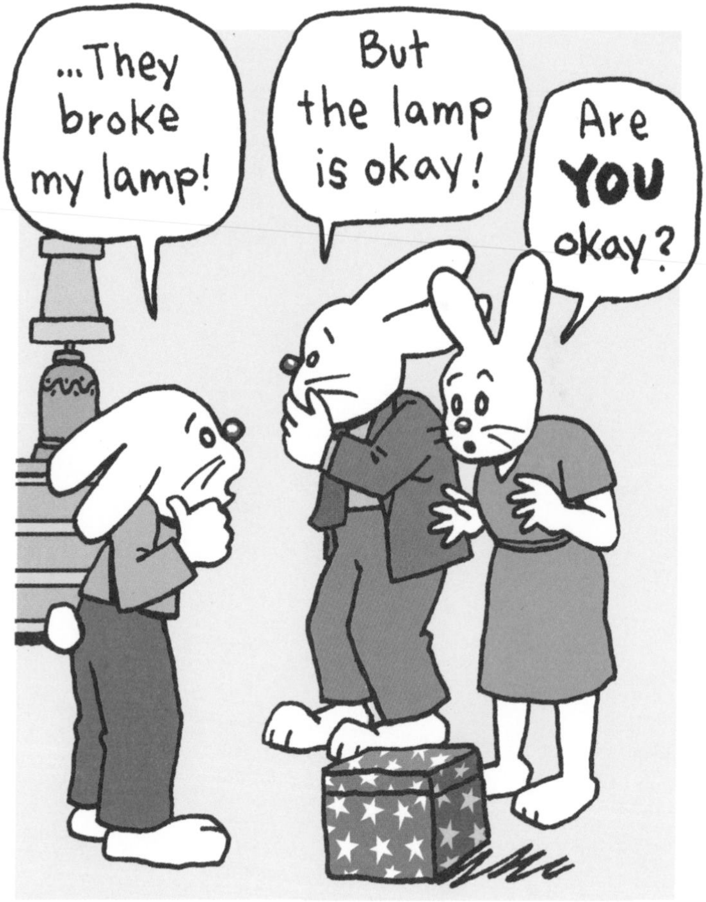
...They broke my lamp!
But the lamp is okay!
Are **YOU** okay?

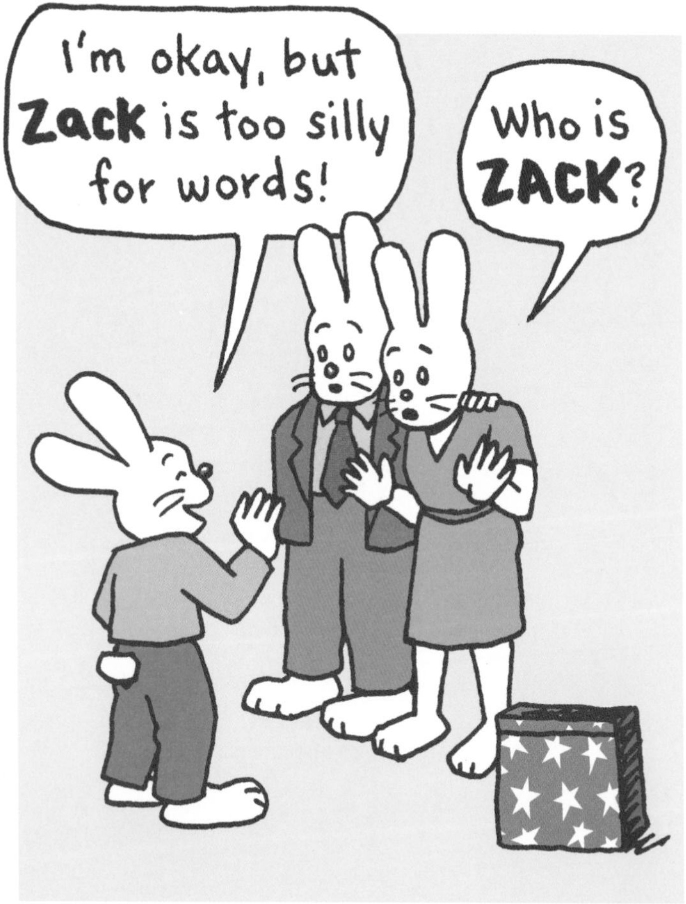
I'm okay, but ZACK is too silly for words!
Who is ZACK?

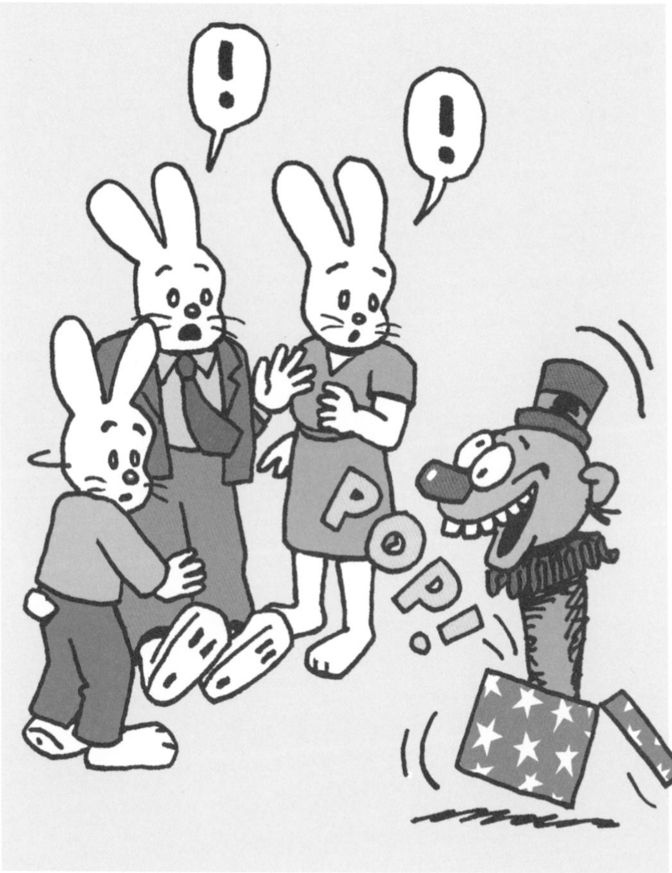
!
!
POP!

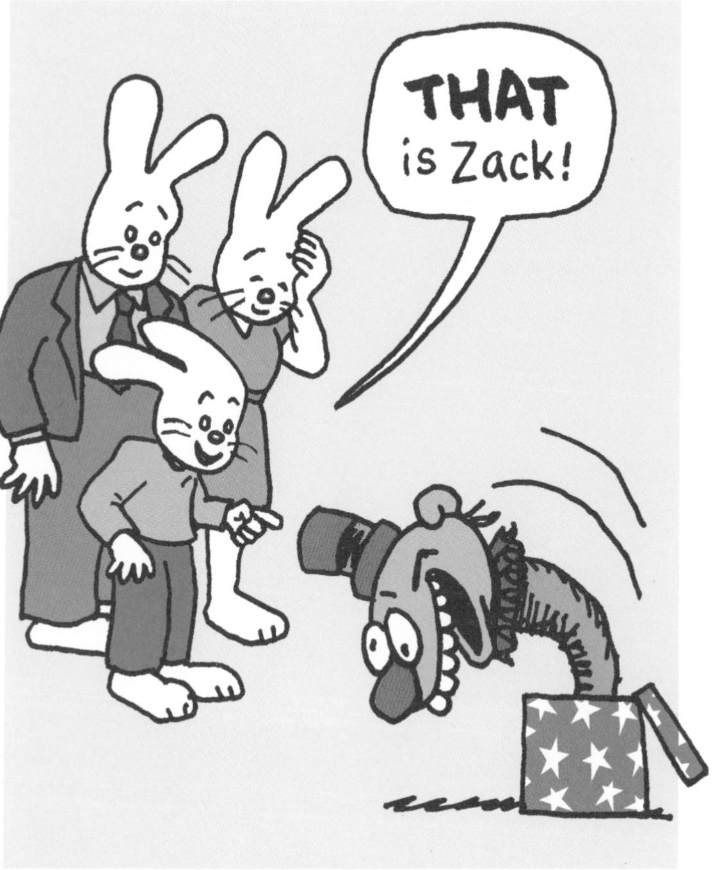
THAT is Zack!

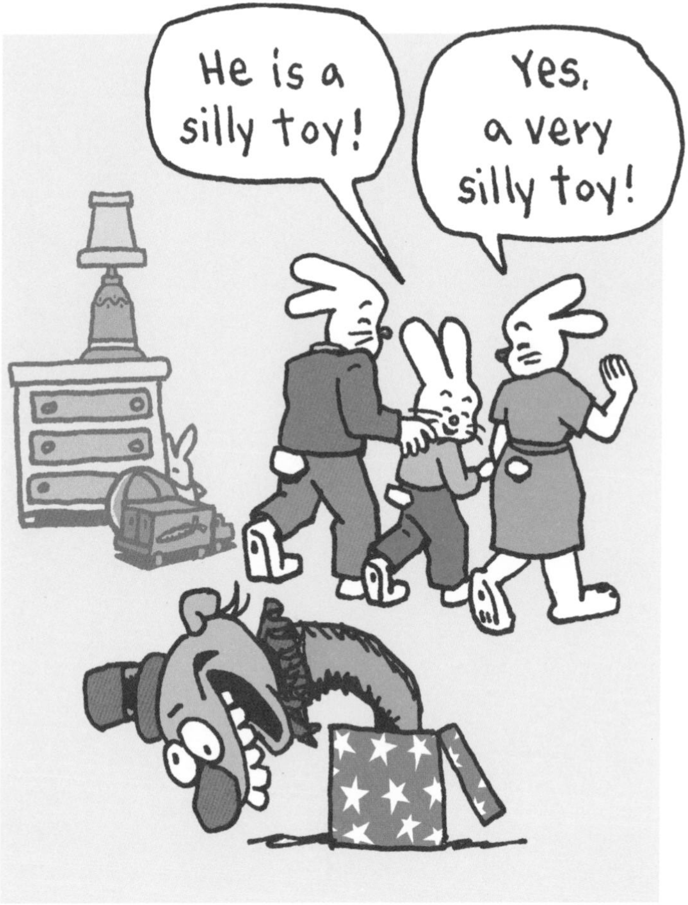
He is a silly toy!
Yes, a very silly toy!

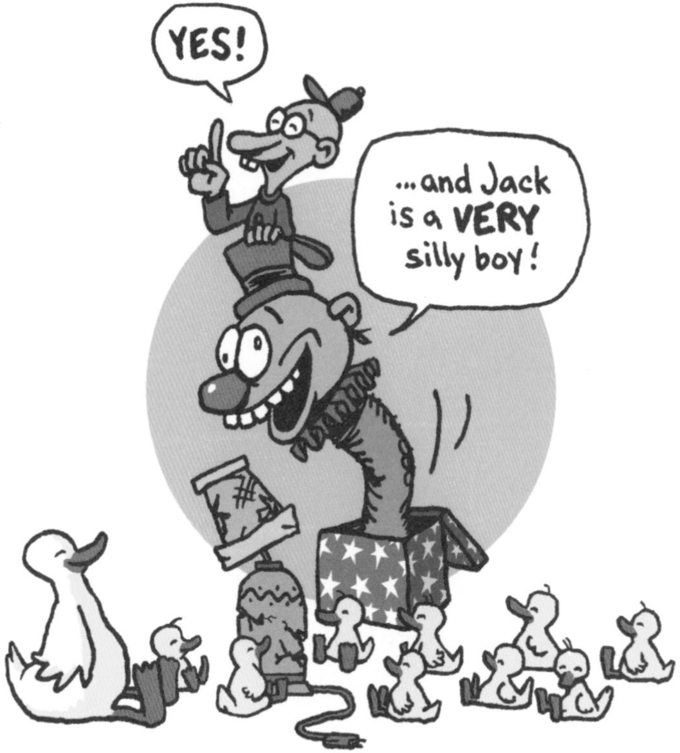
YES!
...and Jack is a VERY silly boy!

# ABOUT THE AUTHOR

**ART SPIEGELMAN** learned to read from looking at comics, "trying to find out if Batman was a Good Guy or a Bad Guy." His now very grownup kids, Nadja and Dash, learned to read from comics, too. He says, "I sacrificed a very valuable collection of old comic books to fatherhood."

He is the author of the Pulitzer Prize winning *MAUS: A Survivor's Tale.* His most recent book for grownups is *Co-Mix: A Retrospective of Comics, Graphics, and Scraps.* His work for children includes the best-selling *Open Me... I'm a Dog!* and the *Little Lit* series of comics anthologies, for which he was both co-editor and contributor. He and his wife, Françoise Mouly, live in New York City. Their cat, Houdini, never learned to read.

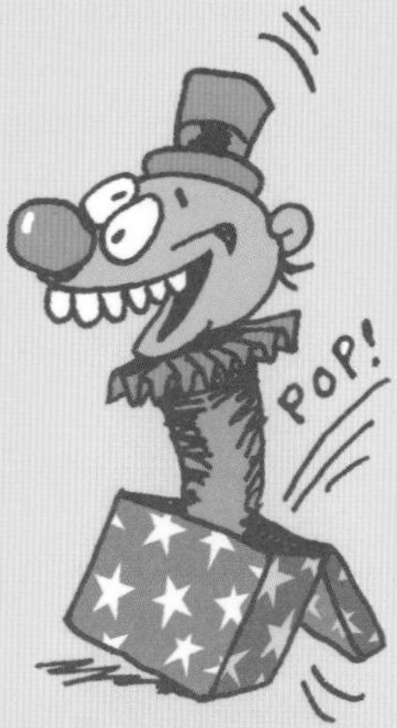
POP!

# HOW TO "TOON INTO READING"

**in a few simple steps:**

Our goal is to get kids reading—and we know kids LOVE comics. We publish award-winning early readers in comics form for elementary and early middle school, and present them in three levels.

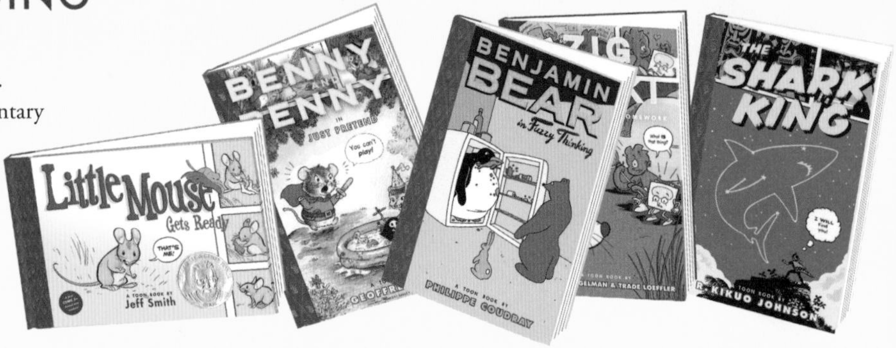

Little Mouse Gets Ready
THAT'S ME!
A TOON BOOK BY Jeff Smith
BENNY AND PENNY
IN JUST PRETEND
You can't play!
BENJAMIN BEAR in Fuzzy Thinking
A TOON BOOK BY PHILIPPE COUDRAY
THE SHARK KING
R. KIKUO JOHNSON


## 1 FIND THE RIGHT BOOK

Veteran teacher Cindy Rosado tells what makes a good book for beginning and struggling readers alike: "A vetted vocabulary, plenty of picture clues, repetition, and a clear and compelling story. Also, the book shouldn't be too easy—or the reader won't learn, but neither should it be too hard—or he or she may get discouraged."

The **TOON INTO READING!™** program is designed for beginning readers and works wonders with reluctant readers.

## 2 GUIDE YOUNG READERS

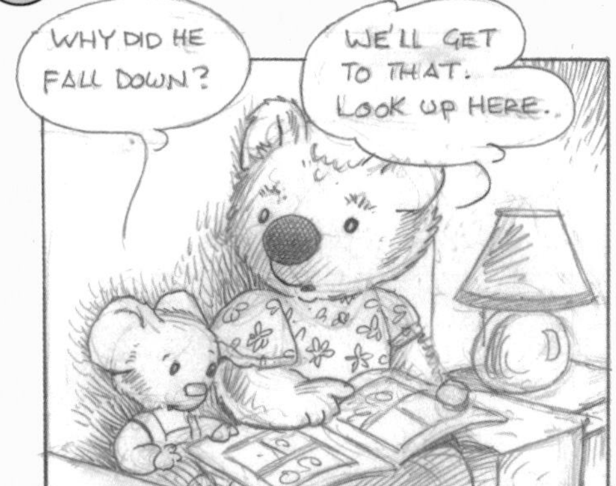

WHY DID HE FALL DOWN?
WE'LL GET TO THAT. LOOK UP HERE.


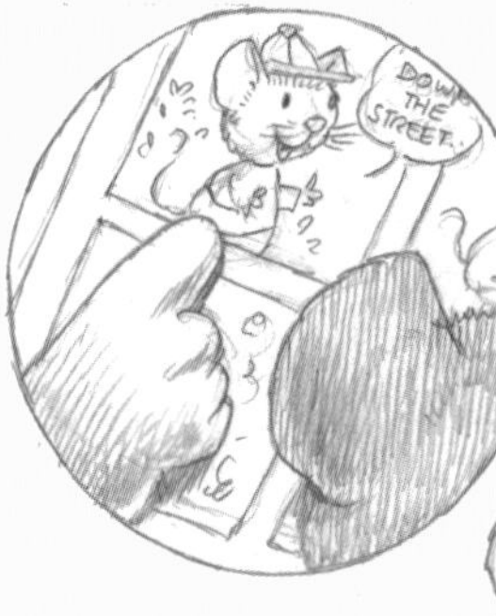

DOWN THE STREET.


**What works?**
Keep your fingertip <u>below</u> the character that is speaking.

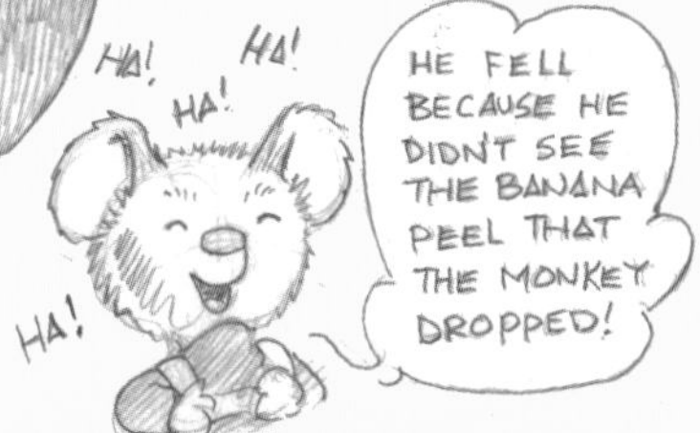

HA! HA! HA! HA!
HE FELL BECAUSE HE DIDN'T SEE THE BANANA PEEL THAT THE MONKEY DROPPED!


## 3 GET OUT THE CRAYONS

Kids see the hand of the author in a comic and it makes them want to tell their own stories. Encourage them to talk, write and draw!